POSTAPOC

"Whether it be poetry, performance art, or prose, Liz Worth has the uncanny ability to turn the grotesque and profane into something sublime and sensual. With *PostApoc* she has taken this to a higher level by solidifying her unique voice and bringing rock 'n roll to its logical dystopian conclusion."

~ Brandon Pitts, author, playwright and poet

POSTAPOC

LIZ WORTH

[N₁ [O₂ [N₁

CANADA

Library and Archives Canada Cataloguing in Publication

Worth, Liz, 1982–, author
PostApoc / Liz Worth.

ISBN 978–1–926942–29–2 (pbk.)

I. Title.

PS8645.O767P68 2013   C813'.6   C2013–903636–9

Printed and bound in Canada on 100% recycled paper.

Now Or Never Publishing
#1101, 1003 Pacific Street
Vancouver, British Columbia
Canada V6E 4P2

nonpublishing.com
Fighting Words.

We acknowledge the support of the Canada Council
for the Arts for our publishing program.

for nightmares

OPEN UP AND START

Outside, the dogs have all gone wild. Can you hear them? Can you feel them down there, voices shaking through loose skin?

At night their jowls fill with thunder. The howling is like wind wringing out hollow moans from the peaks of their spines, a chill that crawls through all the cracks in the windows.

The first time I heard it I thought I'd never heard anything worse. But then I heard the chime of dog tags, ringing beneath lupine shudders. Some of those dogs down there still have their collars on even though they have no homes, no owners anymore because those places, those people, they're all gone now.

So the dogs have all gone wild, reverting back to beasts that run on instinct instead of obedience. They can smell us from all the way up here, they're so hungry.

They've marked all the buildings on the block as their territory, bricks soaked so many times the smell's strong enough to climb the walls.

But those dogs, they don't know we're all starving, too.

Aimee, she's always saying we should do something to get rid of them. Poison or trap them. Wait till they starve and drive knives right between their ribs, plunge blades into their hearts and eat the beasts before they eat us.

But Cam keeps telling her no, says we need to keep the dogs around, that one day they could end up protecting us. He says that, right now, the dogs are all we have. Cam says a lot of things like that.

Before this all happened I thought the sky was going to open up and start spitting out animals. I thought the world would end in blood and hail, in bones and tiny bodies hitting the pavement until everything was pulp and fur.

But it started with the earth sucking all the moisture back into the ground and replacing it with a slow, quiet dread that hung over the city like a veil. It even sucked the water from our bodies, sweat beading along upper lips, leached to the surface by magnetic fields.

The day the drought finally broke, the sky brought down splotches of red, crimson breaking loose from the heavy velvet of clouds gone grey, drops drying to rust on the sidewalks everywhere, like old gum. Anyone caught in the chemical storm melted, just disappeared except for small puddles of sludge and sinew here and there.

But there was more to it than that, of course.

There was that day when all those people's chests imploded. It was in the thick of summer and all the girls had cut their hair or pulled it up into big ponytails, kept it tucked into bandanas or thrift store scarves. It was just too hot to have anything shading your neck, not just that summer, actually, but that whole year.

We only knew one person with air conditioning, so all of our friends invited themselves over to one apartment to get blasted with cold and blasted in every other way, too. That's where I was the day a neighbour from upstairs hopped down the fire escape and told us she'd just seen it herself, walking home along King Street: men and women with chests caved in, blood soaking through thin summer fabrics and eyes filmy and red.

We were never the kind of people who would watch the news, but we did that night, and heard about all this happening in Austin, Tokyo, Berlin, Calcutta, Sydney, Morroco and everywhere else.

I'm pretty sure the taste of my beer changed then, got mixed up with the sweat bubbling up on my lip as I chugged back everything I could swallow, trying to focus on the sound of liquid working behind my ears, pounding it all back as hard as I could to keep any more words from getting into me.

It didn't work, though. No matter what I did, I heard way more than I ever wanted to.

But if anyone thinks it was hard in those days to block anything out, it's nothing compared to how quiet it can get now.

I'm pretty sure it was longer, but it felt like it was just a few months after Aimee and I were in the Market, late afternoon heat gnawing at the backs of our calves. A shadow of smog had covered every city on the continent with a permanent grey, though the sun still fired with a precision focus that cut through the shrouded slabs of sky.

We'd been hearing about molecular shifts, not here but in other cities. It was in New York, Oslo, Stockholm where there were pockets of nothing—space, air—that people walked through and turned to mist, their bodies and bones disintegrating, nothing left but a suspended eyelid or a black speck of pupil.

Scarcity was a new word we were all starting to learn. By then there was a habitual hunger that had us reaching into fruit stands when no one was looking, moving fast through gawking tourists whose optimism seemed almost endless, our bags bulging with stolen apples and pints of strawberries.

In the park I reached into the pocket of my army cutoffs but withdrew my hand quickly with the confusion of a sting, my middle finger slit straight down the middle.

Aimee reached, tore back the flap of my cargo pocket and jiggled until the apple rolled onto the grass. That's when we saw the blade of its stem, the spikes at its base, things we were sure hadn't been there when we'd been dipping our hands into fruit baskets minutes before.

We'd been hearing about food turning to stones, pebbles, in people's mouths. But until then these were all just stories we'd heard—paranoia running wild. Now it was happening to us, my blood real and dark and smeared across the pocket of my shorts.

And I had to try hard not to cry then, even though I wanted to, badly, because that was the day that everything really started to feel too contaminated, like something new was creeping in close, closer, breathing hot darkness against our faces.

All through that year a strange heat had been seeping in slow and low to the ground, turning this city into a body swarmed by flies and clothed in soot that never seemed to exhale long enough to even offer us a sigh of wind.

The walls of buildings would sweat and the roaches in everyone's apartments had grown, thrived. Whole streets of trees bent at the trunks, their bark blackening.

All through that year we tried to remember the last time we had anything we could call a season, and all kept wondering: when did this really start? What was the first moment, the first incident? Was it last year, when summer stretched into November? Was it when all those birds fell from the sky somewhere in Nashville? Did the chemical rain or personal implosions only mean it was already too late?

When did we start thinking of it as The End, pronouncing it with capital letters, somehow making it official?

There were a lot of questions. There was a lot of wondering. We used to wonder about this sort of thing a lot.

We don't wonder about it so much anymore.

SISTERHOOD

Except that's not really true, what I just told you. About wondering. Maybe that part about "we," but I didn't say whether that includes me. It doesn't. Because this thing happened a long while back. This thing that turned me into a held breath, kept my hands shaking for asylum.

People used to see me a certain way. I was a girl who got noticed. Untouchable. Someone people thought they'd never be friends with.

But I'd left town for a while and came back half-dead. A downward spiral bored through my head.

As the sole survivor of a suicide pact I was reduced to panhandling outside of the Mission, just to be able to get in to see a show. I'd grown up in that club, but after I'd left they didn't know how to fit my name on the guest list anymore. There was no glory for the girl who couldn't break on through to the suicide.

The Vapids were playing the night I met Aimee. I'd spent a few hours outside before the doors opened, hands out and an eye on the layers of charms at my neck and wrists. I believed they could—would—bring me luck, power, persuasion. Healing. They clicked at my pulse points, dogs' nails on a hardwood floor.

And maybe I did have some luck that night, because I made enough money to get into the show and enough to buy something extra to dip into.

I don't know how much time passed between getting inside and getting high, but I don't think it was long before I was a writhing OD on the Mission bathroom floor. Later, I'd asked Aimee what it looked like.

"I'd never seen that happen before. The skin. You'd think it'd be hot, flushed. A sick exterior. But it's not. It's chill come alive, barely."

I was disappointed. It sounded the same as what I'd seen in others, a look I'd learned between sets when Valium were still playing, still alive. We all liked to tease our bodies to a metronome brink in those days. It was what the cult of the music dictated.

At that Vapids show, though, I hadn't planned on taking it very far. Hadn't expected the shit to hit me so hard, so fast.

In the bathroom the ceiling was fogged with pot smoke. I couldn't see anyone's faces but I knew other girls were around. I could hear their shrieking laughter. I tried to talk but my mouth was broken. All I could do was sink deeper into the base of the old velour couch, something that once would have been expensive, plush, now balding trash against a toilet stall. My eyes spun, pinwheeled. A silver spool of saliva tore out of the side of my mouth.

And then I was suddenly light enough to fit across a pair of arms. My shallow bones. I could hear the straw of my hair against skin, my head a bleached explosion at the inside of an elbow. I could smell myself. The same white Smiths t-shirt I always wore stained with a dozen other nights. Its blooms of sweat released below the nose.

Aimee kept me floating by asking me questions: what did you take/who did you get it from/where do you live/do you want to go home or to the hospital/do you remember what you did earlier today/do you remember who you are?

Not that I had to tell her my name. She already knew. "I've seen you around before," she said. "You're Ang. You're Ang. You're Ang." She said it for me, in case I didn't know it anymore. She recognized me, the way I believed people still should, or would, even though I'd chopped my hair from waist-length to boy-short, bleached it from black to bare-bulb white. My weight had stayed off, though, cheekbones and chin still sharp, jutting.

I could never remember this part, but Aimee told me later I threw up in the sink as soon as we got to my place. Light purple pulp and cigarette ash in the shared bathroom at the end of the hall.

I kept the door to my room unlocked, having lost my key a month before and not bothered to ask for a replacement. I had nothing left that I cared about anyway—the life lesson of depression.

My bed filled most of the apartment because the place was really just a room with a closet. Every other inch of it was covered in plaid shirts and bras, a rough pair of jeans I'd stolen and never worn. With the sleeve of her flannel shirt, Aimee wiped the residue from around my mouth and cleared a space on the floor all in the same motion.

She pulled me down and I pulled a piece of chalk off the windowsill behind her and drew a circle on the floor. I slid a ring off my finger and dropped it into the circle's center, pronounced us blood sisters. She accepted my sisterhood. For weeks after I would ask her to tell me this story, over and over, as affirmation that someone wanted me close, that someone had wanted to save me.

Aimee stayed with me for a while after that. I didn't own a blanket, relied only on the clothes piled on the mattress to keep us covered.

Aimee said she hardly slept at all whenever she stayed over. She learned early on that I lacked margins when I slept, a desiccated portrait.

The remains of my past were fossilized on the bedroom walls. Above us a suicide scene played out, all the way from the west coast. The room spat Polaroids and memories in negative images, a high contrast inversion in frosted blues to match the lips of my dead boyfriend, his dead friends.

The story always ended the same, with me being the only one to walk away.

That's where that story ended, and my question of responsibility began: was that the first moment, the first incident that jarred the universe off its course?

Did we lose the first rhythm because I didn't die that day? I can't even remember what dropped off in the beginning: the rush of mornings, maybe. Traffic and alarm clocks and packed subway trains. Not that I ever had a job to go to. Or a routine to maintain.

If I'd died that day, would we still have the rhythm of the seasons? We lost the silk of leaf on leaf in spring wind. We lost the colour green and forgot that branches used to be something more than spider-long fingers that snap in frail air. We lost the stop and start of red lights, green lights, and the caution of yellow. We lost caution. We lost birds at dawn and bus schedules and daily newspapers, the timing of rain after a storm's first thunderclap and any predictable rise of the sun. We lost, and we lost, and we lost.

And as we lost, people wondered not only where it started, but how, and why. Was it pollution? Germ warfare? Greed? God?

And as they wondered, my conviction grew, intuition tracing everything back to that one day when the knife didn't go deep enough, and I thought then that I knew the answer.

MULTIPLE CHOICE

Before The End I used to wake up to the following options. Choose the answer that best fits your current state of mind:

a) Reckless
b) Moderately depressed
c) Mildly euphoric
d) Uninhibited
e) All of the above

That was during a time when everyone wanted to join a suicide cult. I can't explain it now, and I don't think I ever could, or cared enough to question it. It just made sense back then.

I swear to you that we all walked around with a similar conversation stuck in our heads, like music:

Friend 1: Well, I guess I should let you go for now.

Friend 2: Okay, I'm going to go kill myself later anyway.

Friend 1: Cool. So I'll see you tonight?

Friend 2: See you tonight.

We obsessed over self-destruction because that's just what you did in those days. Even if they didn't want to admit it, there were so many people who were ready to die. It was romance for a jaded generation.

Valium gave us the soundtrack, the commandments, the first being that living as close to death as possible was the only way to really live. This showed us all our true priorities.

I especially thought their lyrics were written psychically, with me in mind, as if the band knew I'd been waiting for something else aside from the boredom of my parents' love, the awkward hugs and the lack of danger/destruction/detonation. And feeling safe is no way to feel alive.

Valium taught me to embrace depression as the essence of my personality, my natural way of being. They taught me to cut out anyone who didn't want to know the real me. Through Valium I went feral, seethed where I was formerly subdued.

Valium had a following starting from their very first show, and hooked and hypnotized and hauled in everyone who saw them. The audience knew they were part of something. You could feel a movement, a true underground coming together. The kind of thing someone would write a book about twenty years later.

From the start Valium had a ritual: to communally explore desires for death. Keeping danger on our breaths, the music led us all to discard responsibilities, conventional processes, high expectations. The projection of a skull behind the stage matched the skulls worn by fans. The projection was meant as a visual power thought. The ones who understood the band knew it was real. They could admit their desires and succumb to psychic process. Older generations—reporters, parents, bar owners—dismissed it all as gimmick. They didn't believe in suicide pacts or mass cults, just thought we were doing it for fashion. The only ones who knew the truth were the ones who mattered. Valium made sure all their fans knew they mattered.

Valium had another ritual: to create images and texts that contained sigils—power thoughts and spells. They'd form a circle, let their beliefs permeate the bonds between them. There were no chants or blood sacrifices or stones, only energy pushed onto images and texts that held the band's words and music and photographs.

They created sigil-born spirits by distributing the images at their shows and on the streets. They glued posters to the sides of buildings and told everyone to keep the images somewhere they could be seen at all times. The more eyes on the images the more their power grew.

Valium's music constantly invoked energies this way. But to hear the band properly you needed to be part of their mass hallucinations. Kids who lived out of town ran away from home to squat in the city so they wouldn't miss a show.

I wasn't one of these kids, but I wanted to be. I used to pretend my parents didn't care where I slept. Convinced myself I was unwanted, an orphan. Told lies about my past, re-imagined my story until it held heaps of criticism, abuse. I thought it sounded better. Aroused sympathy.

My stories sounded a lot like the ones I heard from other kids I met. We liked that about each other. My stories sounded so true I started to believe them.

It didn't matter if anyone knew I was lying, as it wouldn't take long for my real life to catch up with my fake life anyway; what I've piled on myself, it's been enough. Ask Aimee.

My eighteen-year-old body quivered when I first met Hunter. He was all grey eyeliner and long black hair. A blue light on the club's dancefloor caught the thin silver loop in his nose. Valium wasn't playing that night but they were there, out to support. On the bill were White Eagle and Girl and some other band from out of town none of us had heard of before.

We were at the bar, buying a drink. Hunter caught me staring at him and smiled. Asked if I was old enough to order anything more than a pop.

I had ID that said I was. I'd stolen it from a friend's older sister, who thought she'd lost her license. Hunter didn't wait for me to answer though. He ordered for both of us, clinked his glass to mine before we took our first taste. He said, "I've seen you around before," and I felt my life colliding into this one moment, everything building up to make me into the person I wanted to be, which was really just a person who was wanted by someone important. Or just a person who was wanted.

His favourite colour was green. His speaking voice was the same as his singing voice. He had a dark scar behind his ear where a homemade tattoo had gone wrong.

He liked to run his hand over my stomach, said that's where my skin was softest. Every time his fingers grazed my navel my ankles quaked, which seemed reason enough for us to move in together two months after we met. Or it was more like me leaving home to live with him in a house he shared with the rest of his band and whoever else needed a place to crash in or pass through.

There was more of a fight from my parents than I wanted. I had to push their voices out of my head the night I picked through my bag of clothing, making small piles of jeans and t-shirts on the floor because Hunter didn't have enough hangers to share with me.

I had to push their voices out of my head again the third or fourth night as I got into bed—a mattress on the floor, black unwashed sheets gritty with something like sand—and felt the room around me take on a different meaning then, something more permanent than I'd ever felt before.

There were other girls in the house, tentative cats who threw me suspicious eyes and toughened shoulders. Eventually the band would all have girlfriends, but at first some of them just had girls—different faces on regular rotation unwilling to share their territory. I wouldn't understand that feeling until much, much later.

I was supposed to go back to high school that year. I'd kind of stopped going the year before and only had a few credits to go before I could graduate. Instead, I'd lie on the living room floor in that house, head to head with Hunter, stereo on, acid on our tongues, letting the wrong things into us. Even at the time I think I knew there was a mistake being made, but it felt too good to stop, and it felt too fast to be anything but irreversible. Who need-ed high school when I was already going beyond the beyond, feeling that the future shimmered in awe, waiting for me to walk right into it on Hunter's arm?

The other girls in the house got used to me because they had to. The stones in their expressions eventually fell away, replaced with something kinder, softer.

We all knew, without ever saying it, that Valium's obsessions had infiltrated each of us in the same way. We had welfare and didn't ever have anywhere to be—no jobs, no homes—but our heads were overwhelmed with the obligation of having to wake up every day.

Together, me and the other girls started to spend our after-noons (we were never up before one o'clock) in copy shops, pho-tocopying pocket-sized flyers for the next Valium shows. We popped pink gum as the machines whirred and then we'd bring our stacks of paper back to the house to cut, pile and admire before handing them out to anyone who looked like they might be one of us. If the band was playing out of town a couple hours away, we'd take a bus and expand the web, build the cult.

The more Valium pushed, the further things went, until we were all the way out in Vancouver. The move out there was fast. The guys had heard they might be able to make it bigger on the west coast and wanted to try it for at least a few months and see. We left the house with some friends and immediately reminded ourselves of the truths we had, each one sung in Hunter's voice, written on his tongue, the pressure of which kept dipping into self-destruction for inspiration. But our tolerance had gotten so high that Valium had to go to another level if they wanted to write more songs. It was a weight they'd never experienced before, and it got under the hoods of their eyes, soaked into their lids and drew them down, down, down.

And so the pact. A promise. To go together. It wasn't so much that nothing was going as planned (though I am the only one who holds that truth, and it's cut into my hands so deeply I'm barely able to carry it all the time), but that Valium *was* the plan.

Truth: when you set out to design your own demise, you find that your vision is quite easily attained.

Truth: the moment you question it is the moment you know you can't turn anything around.

Truth: I didn't regret it or question it at all at the time. At least not before Hunter's blade sunk into me.

Pact: we agreed that there was no escape. That we had all committed to a lifetime of voices, of off-white anxiety and nameless red fury.

Pact: roses and leather jackets. Dress for the ceremony of pills and deep cuts.

Scene: "You and me." Those were the words Hunter uttered after we swallowed our doses, which were meant more to keep us calm than to kill us. The death would come with a blade between bone, pushed in long and deep from wrist to elbow. Everyone back then used to talk about how that was the "right way to do it." So we all paired off, to help each other, to hold each other, to become a Valium song come to life in death.

Hunter and the guys had all discussed it: they would each slit one of their own wrists first so we, the girlfriends, would know they were serious. They didn't want to be questioned, disbelieved.

They would then cut into us girls, and then make the final slices into their own arms. We'd all been warned we might have to help, though, either with ourselves or with them. "There will be a lot of blood," they'd said. "The knife handle will be slippery in your hand."

Wet rust on grey carpet. No recollection of whose knife was the first to sink in, or whose blood spilled fastest. Later, in dreams I'd have only after drinking red wine, I'd remember that someone cried out at one point, but that I had my back to the others, my body in Hunter's arms, and I didn't want to turn around.

Before we started, I'd told Hunter I wanted to do the second cut myself. I'd never accomplished anything before and this was my last chance to try to get something right.

But he said no, that he'd cut into me both times because he didn't think I'd have the strength to go deep enough. I've always wondered if he kept the cuts shallow on purpose.

I've always wondered how many times I'll wish that he hadn't. Or how many times I'll wish I could have actually finished what he started.

- 4 -
MY USUAL WAY

The End's endless summer was relentless, made us peel from anywhere we sat. It followed us into every corner, every moment.

Nothing stayed white in all that heat. No such feeling as clean anymore as the streets stayed spattered, the chemical contagion and evaporations continued.

Viruses spread through tap water. Norwalk and rota. C Difficile. The lake water was overrun with flushed prescriptions, antibiotic residue passed through urine. Bacterial defense mechanisms strengthened, developed immunities we could not. The treatment system was caught off guard, unprepared for the imbalance of bad medicine. Gastrointestinal outbreaks came in waves, stomach and intestinal linings in constant distress. They said it could take years to develop the right water treatment. It was something they'd never prepared for. We didn't have years to wait, so instead we learned to collect rainwater between rations handed out in jugs outside City Hall. It was the first thing we had to start lining up for. We were told it was from an emergency stockpile, that we had to use it sparingly.

We were told the city wasn't sure how long supplies would last, or whether other cities would be able to help. The problem was everywhere, they said, and some places were worse off already. Niagara Falls was over, decimated; that place hadn't been running on anything but illusion anyway. No one was really surprised to hear the news.

Here, the rations weren't enough. Unwilling to let go of old comforts, people wanted to shower, bathe, cook, clean, so they used the tap water despite the risks, smearing their floors and counters and bodies with germs, never understanding how viruses spread. "If we can't see it, then it can't be real," their collective conscious confirmed. Induce vomiting. Cramps, bloating, diarrhea, nausea, fever. Secondary symptoms: paranoia. The city's corneas had turned the colour of viscera, its winds a deep beige. Grains of contamination stained everything and anything you touched was coated in microscopic illness, flecks of shit and puke.

We forgot what it felt like to be anything but filthy. Clean wasn't even a concept anymore. Eventually we also forgot about television and glossy magazines and newspapers. Forgot about shopping for new clothing or shoes or records. Forgot about apples, oranges, plums, about peaches and fresh red peppers. Forgot about money and the luxury of new things.

But we remembered scarcity. Understood it, finally, through the standard-issue care packages, brown sacks of whatever could be spared, not just water now but thin bars of soap, bandaids, tampons, peanut butter sometimes, or canned beans. We heard food supplies came from emergency reserves that would eventually run out. We heard no answers about what would happen after that.

City grocery stores only had about three days' worth of food at the best of times; shelves here stayed empty, doors locked, lights off.

We heard some cities were better off than others, though; that Montreal still had electricity fifty percent of the time, that some European cities like Paris had set up community kitchens in city squares where they had massive cookouts over bonfires.

But Montreal was too far and Paris was only a rumour, so we stayed with what we knew. I just dealt with it all in my usual way anyway: by staying drunk, scavenging pills. Kept my hand out constantly even though I knew it would make me sick again in a few days.

Everyone was floating around then. No one knew what to do. The roads were always lined up, jammed with people leaving, thinking that if they got out, got somewhere open and northern, it would all be okay.

But smaller towns weren't helping out the big cities much. They weren't even letting newcomers in. People were driving north, hoping to be saved, and being told to turn around. No one had enough to share. Whole neighbourhood blocks succumbed to spontaneous combustion.

The rest of us just crashed around, too sick and uneasy to stay settled, believing that we'd all be led somewhere else at some point soon. I was okay with this, used to the in-between. The feeling I used to call "figuring things out" became the norm.

Confession: we'd been waiting for the world to end. Believed it would be Our Time. We—meaning us, our friends, our familiar faces—believed ourselves to be ready for this, whatever that meant. Remember, it was a scene. A cult of death teasers. What had started with Valium continued with Shit Kitten, who rose up to fill the gap on the circuit after Valium's decomposition. Shit Kitten showed us how to spend nights lighting fires at the backs of our throats.

There was—still is—a guy named Tooth. Not a nickname; something he always insisted was more serious than that, a name he'd picked for himself when he joined Shit Kitten, the band's philosophy being that we all have two choices: be what the world decides you'll be, or be what you want to be, and he wanted to be Tooth and his singer was Rattail. Self-made, Tooth called it.

We were drinking outside the back door of the Mission when he asked me if I ever thought of myself that way, but I didn't really know how to answer because everything he talked about sounded too much like being alive and I only knew deconstruction. I felt embarrassed then, like Tooth would feel too much of a distance between us to keep talking to me, but he did keep talking, about how Shit Kitten doesn't think of what they do as songwriting, that they instead create inverted rituals, channel confessions that don't come from the band but from the audience.

"We want to rip you all apart, starting from your insides." I remember that exact phrase because he took out a ballpoint pen and wrote those words on the white toe of my black high tops.

It sounded like a bad thing but Tooth said it wasn't, that it was communal. When people go see a band they're all there for the same reasons. Shows are ritualistic. Remove the sound but keep the movement and you're witnessing something tribal. A new force in the room.

Tooth took my hand in his mouth. The fire in my throat had made me manic so I let him take my tongue, too. His teeth were stunted yellow cubes, lips reluctant around mine even though his hand tugged at the back of my bra.

After he'd told me all about himself it was time to go back in, time for the show to start. I'd given him nothing except a little tongue, but still he wanted me to follow him into the Mission. We stood up and the alley swerved. The fire's flames were licking all the way down my esophagus. "Whatever happens, Shit Kitten's taking all our fans with us. You're in the club now," he said.

Inside, Aimee stood tall in electric blue heels. Bare legs and a mini in November. Above her ankle was a scratch that could have been dirt. She let me climb on her back so I could see the stage over the heads of mutant boys. She shivered under me every time my hair poked into the back of her neck. I breathed for her through the oval of my mouth as Shit Kitten drew a ritual around us, built a song called "PostApoc" up and up until we believed its presence would blanket us. People leaned back on their heels, daring to faint into the absolute faith in what they were hearing: that The End would be easy, especially if you wanted it to be.

"*It's my body and I'll die if I want to,*" the band sang. And we answered back, because we wanted it, had been feeling it teem in the heat and repression for years. Even though the city was quivering all around us, we felt far away from it, felt like if it touched us we were ready anyway.

It's my body and I'll die if I want to.

WHAT WE BELIEVED

It only took seven Shit Kitten shows for their new world order to become embedded in me. Each syllable sung was a microchip inserted, a dart aimed at the heart.

I'd been gone a while from my one-room apartment. No one ever let me stay anywhere too long. I brought too many ghosts and never enough rent money.

Before it all got really bad I was staying at a friend's place. Sandy. A dancer. I can't remember her real name now, just her stage name. Just another face I'd met hanging out at the Mission.

We hadn't been friends long when I started crashing with her. The redemption Shit Kitten brought me lasted about as long as I did in Sandy's apartment. Meaning a few weeks maybe.

I got home from the Mission the night it all came together. All I had to do was fall asleep on the couch, and then:

THE NEW WORLD ORDER: A PRELUDE

When the last day is written the world will hold up two pages and they will say SHIT KITTEN. *And you will stand around us, grinning with teeth that could cut out stars.*

THE REAL NEW WORLD ORDER: A (WO)MANIFESTO

This is not a conspiracy, but a leveling, a cleansing. When the New World emerges, only the strongest will remain.

The only way to get there is now. If you like to be looked at, go get looked at. If you like to be high, help other people get high, too. These are the ways we will survive, by absorbing the oldest means and using them and knowing them and exploiting them. The only structural pyramid left behind will be the one that has always been in place, the one SOCIETY *chooses to ignore. The one that barely needs to be* SPOKEN *because* IF YOU DON'T KNOW, WE'RE NOT TELLING.

THIS WORLD WILL CHEW YOU UP AND SHIT YOU OUT.
And so:
It's my body and I'll die if I want to.
But hang on a bit longer. Because you are not alone. WE ARE NOT ALONE.
~~Make an informed and smart choice.~~ BE SMART AND INFORMED BECAUSE THERE WILL NOT BE A CHOICE. *There will only be basic instinct and the muscles in your legs to carry you when* THE END *comes. And it will, oh yes, it will.*
Possible psychological effects could include: GUILT, ANXIETY, DEPRESSION, SUICIDAL TENDENCIES.
Guaranteed psychological effects include: ALCOHOL AND DRUG ABUSE.
Possible physical effects could include: LIFE OR DEATH.
Somewhere in there you'll say yes.
P.S. IT'S MY BODY AND I'LL DIE IF I WANT TO.

Sandy woke me up, drunk on vodka. She wanted me to drink with her and I couldn't say no, not with all this new knowledge I had in me.

We blacked in and out, tore the phone out of the wall as we went blind on alcohol, convinced voices were coming through the receiver.

"Introvert," one voice said.

"Suffer sufferer suffer," came another.

"You are inversions."

We thought these were the voices of people who'd been dying in the streets from the chemical rain, their bodies turned to water and travelling through the wires and cables that ran deep into the earth.

With one foot against the wall Sandy curled black nails under the phone. I wrapped my arms around her waist and ONE, TWO, THREE we pulled until the phone broke free, the wall spitting cords from the hole left behind. Then, from the balcony, we watched as the phone broke against the parking lot seven floors below.

The phone booth at the corner was so hot that the dark wads of gum on the floor were peeling off the pavement. We had to deal with it because it was our only connection afterwards. None of the neighbours would let us in to make a call.

The toe of my running shoe nudged one spot back and bright pink Bubblelicious peeked from underneath the dirty skin. I remember that better than the conversation I had with my mother. Now all the words are mixed up, mangled. Some parts of what I remember are true, but most of them aren't.

I wish I'd been able to hold onto the words as they came through the phone, because I know the way I hear them in my head is all wrong.

ME: Hi, mom.

MOM: Ang, hi. How are you?

ME: Good. How are you?

MOM: Fine. Dad's fine. We're both fine. Except we don't think you are.

ME: Why?

MOM: Ang, I can hear you smoking. You're blowing smoke right into the phone.

ME: So?

MOM: So how can you afford cigarettes when you aren't even working?

ME: It's just, well, I find a way. I have to. They're all that gets me through the day sometimes.

MOM: —

ME: And, well, I find it hard to get out of bed some days. A lot of days actually.

MOM: —

ME: Maybe I can come over one night. Stay for a weekend, even just on the couch or something. Where it'll be quiet. Because there are days when I feel like these voices are inside me.

MOM: —

ME: But it's too loud. Everywhere's too loud, especially the places I stay. But the voices are trying to tell me something, and I think maybe if I hear them, they'll go away. It's never quiet enough, though, not even in my head.

MOM: Those sleeping pills you're taking make you look like shit.

ME: I know. They cut crescent moons under my eyes, across the tops of my cheeks.

MOM: If you come over, I could hold you. You'd sleep then, if you let yourself in between my arms.

ME: —

MOM: Well, why don't you let us know when you're going to come visit? Maybe you could come this weekend.

ME: Well, yeah, this weekend's possible, but see, the thing is I'm a bit short on cash. I might not even have enough for bus fare to get out there.

MOM: I'm sure we can get your Dad or your brother to come pick you up.

ME: Uh, okay, but couldn't you and Dad just send me cash before then? Even just fifty bucks or something?

I haven't talked to her since. That feels like it was a long time ago now.

- 6 -
DISINTEGRATION

We really knew it was The End when the fires were no longer contained to our throats and the ghosts got into the margins of the night. Flames had found their way to the city, engulfed entire streets, gated communities, high rise buildings. The biggest mistake people made was believing the government would take care of them, that "they" or "someone" or "something" would stop this from happening before it got too bad.

But the people running things were just as scared and useless as the rest of us, caught off guard and left with no answers. They told us they could only do so much for so long. They were all dying, too, disappearing or combusting or dehydrating from dysentery. They told us they could not change fate, and fate was bringing us to the downfall.

My friends and I were lucky in a way, because we were never enough of a part of society to expect anyone would want to take care of us anyway. We knew better.

From the corner of any eye were other people like us, maybe, lost or moving on or running from something. They were mostly grey movement, so it was hard to tell. Cars were still hulking for miles along the road, but this time some people would never end up getting out of them. For weeks afterwards you'd see their bodies rotting inside. Stubborn corpses. Other drivers' seats sat empty, keys still in the ignition, passengers sliced into disintegration.

I was with Aimee. We'd been popping pills all night, that last night of what was left of the world as we'd known it. The only drugs we could find were something new that could numb and stimulate simultaneously. Aimee's guy had picked them up. We both had lovers then—not boyfriends, just guys with faces as temporary as our feelings. They had names like blank slates: Smith and English.

The problem with the pills was they'd melt into your eyes. And in that heat, that fire, everything was a squint already.

The city sucked in every sound, cushioned us in deafness. There was no patterned footfall, no breaking windows, no screams. Even the flames were whispers diminished.

Only once did a sound break through the insulating void: a sob, quick and unrestrained. Horror, it held, so I let the pills spread from my eyes to my ears, clouding my head in powder.

My ankles, shins, knees lost their tendons and bones. They rolled over the pavement, which had all turned to rubber. So high, I thought the soles of my shoes were melting against the ground. I bent over to untie them and the street rose up to catch me, lay me on my side. Smith's hands scooped me up a few times, big hooks curled up in my armpits. I only knew they were there because his hands were so fast and hard that the next day, black rings of bruise rippled out from underneath the sleeve of my t-shirt.

In bare feet I felt every pebble and piece of glass on the ground, but at the time it didn't hurt. It was too hot for shoes. I held onto them with curled fingers but they dropped from my hands and broke the sound barrier. The clapping sounds they made on the ground skittered up and over the rooftops around us.

We'd all been walking around with backpacks, bulging purses for a while before then. In those days no one ever left what they needed at home because we didn't know if there'd be a home to go back to later on. We all felt The End coming so we carried what we could, what we loved.

That last night I wore a black faux-fur jacket. My only jacket. It hadn't been cold in what felt like years but I held onto it, just in case. My underarms soaked the lining. My cheekbones shone with sweat. I could see them from my lower peripheries.

Aimee asked why I didn't just take it off, ditch it. I wanted to tell her I might need it, but I had just pushed another pill between my teeth and my throat was raw-dry from the city's fever. I had to wait through the melt of bitter before I could work up enough saliva. When the pill got past my tongue it clung to my throat, sat like a stone.

On Sherbourne Street a house shrugged and yawned, its front door wide open and an old red carpet flashed from its insides like a tongue. Its frame was aloof and unattached and right there for us to take, at least for a night.

From under the push of English's boot on its wooden porch step came a creak that was almost a cry, a surprised sound like the house had forgotten what it was like to have someone walk into it.

Inside the air was a shade cooler, the walls panting something musty and anxious, a brushing of mold over top of the ash and sweat on our skin.

"Shhh," English said. "There's someone here."

He went off into another room, where we heard him call out. "Hello?"

"Hi," Aimee answered. It was the first time we'd laughed all night.

Smith flicked a light switch up and down, even though we knew it wouldn't work. All the streetlights were out, power fried.

There was the aqua taint of Zippo fluid and then the sound of a thumb striking it once, twice, and then we had light. And twenty heads, bald and shining, stared back at us, yellow reflections of the burning lighter fluid bouncing from the sides of their skulls.

"What the fuck." The sentiment strung between us.

English, relieved, sighed for everyone. The place was full of mannequins.

Aimee pulled out a smoke, lit it off Smith's Zippo, and said, "You'll waste good fluid like that, you know."

Later, we lay back on the floor in the room to the right. There were no mannequins in there, just a couch and some mirrors, a filing cabinet in the corner. No one wanted to claim the couch for themselves, so instead we'd taken the cushions off to share as pillows.

Kiss at midnight, me and Smith, lips closed, hard wax against front teeth. We guessed it might have been that time. We hadn't known anyone with a working watch for weeks and we'd forgotten about calendars, days of the week. We guessed it might have been New Year's Day.

Aimee figured the person who'd lived in that house must've made their own clothes or something, used the mannequins for models. English made a joke no one laughed at: "I can think of some other reasons," but could hardly get the words out. His voice was getting thick with the pills we'd dipped into to help us settle in.

Aimee might've said, "You're a pig." At least she could still talk after eating pills all day.

Something dry scuttled across the bare floors upstairs. A second later it was followed by a heavy drag.

"Holy shit," I said. I breathed, but barely. Those two words seemed so small they'd needed claws to pull themselves out of my throat.

English stood, asked, "What do you think is upstairs?"

Smith stood too, asked, "You want me to go check that out with you?"

Aimee started to get up. I was hoping to just pass out. Useless. Aimee said, "You can't both go up there. We need one of you here. Ang is almost out."

English and Smith didn't want to go alone. My fingers went to my lips, shoving something hard between them again, not even thinking about it anymore. My mouth was white sand but somehow I swallowed past it, got the pill down. I held up a hand in the dark. Aimee answered the silhouette, plucked the pill from my fingers, swallowed. Cat's eyes, we had.

Aimee lowered herself back down to the floor as English and Smith went upstairs. Both of us then, giggling. I might have started it, saying, "Oooohhh . . . . spooky. OoooOoooOoooh . . ."

Aimee was mellowing. "It's probably just a raccoon or something," she reasoned. English was laughing, too, then, said he'd probably be knocked out on that last dose before he even got upstairs. His words came to us with the creak of the first few steps.

Right then, the speeding side of the pill kicked in for another dose. I didn't think I'd be able to fall asleep that night. Or maybe ever again. My body was all adrenaline and heartbeat. I looked up the stairs. Smith and English were higher on the steps, taunting ghosts now, too.

"Ooooooohhhhhh," Aimee and I answered back, and then the drugs kicked off a caramel ribbon and sent it running through our voices, something sweet enough that I could close my eyes and nearly believe we were just playing games.

Upstairs, English and Smith's boots scuffed against wood. As the old floorboards squeaked under the curve of their feet I breathed, closed my eyes, and then, somehow, I slept.

I dreamt of Saturn and its rings, the whole planet fallen loose from the stars and hanging low over the intersection two blocks down. Around its waist, brass and blade reflected the city lights. Street lamps and neon glow bounced back so bright that Saturn could have been the sun, disguised for centuries. And those rings, they were so big and bright and bursting with heat, bursting through the window, that for a second that dream came true: Saturn's rings *were* right outside my window. And even though it'd been hot for days with the humidity slinking around our ankles, Saturn's heat was clean, something we could almost accept.

If the next day was really the first day of January, as we'd guessed, it didn't look like it. There was no snow, no cold. By then, the sky had slipped into a coma and the seasons had disappeared altogether.

And so had half the city, half the country, half the world. It was the biggest disappearance yet. People were just suddenly gone, and so were Smith and English.

Aimee and I couldn't stop saying, "They just aren't up there."

We'd looked in every room, looked outside, walked the block and then done the search all over again. And again. And again. It hurt so much to walk I eventually had to crawl. My feet were black from walking barefoot, could've been charred.

Aimee said, "It can't be a joke. They wouldn't joke like this, not for this long."

And even though I knew it was true, I didn't want to hear her say it. But I couldn't tell her that, because the depth of silence behind those words was even worse. I needed Aimee's voice beside me because there didn't seem to be anything else. There wasn't even anything left of them. No blood, no bodies, just gone.

We wondered if anyone we knew remained. We wondered if we were the last.

It didn't take us long to find out we weren't.

- 7 -
THIS IS HOW WE LIVE

If you want quiet, go outside. There's no prowl of motors, no stress of brakes. No lawnmowers or blaring stereos. This street is as empty as all the others. Oh, there are other people around of course, just a lot fewer than there were before. If we're still here, there have to be others, except they're all reduced to brutal instinct and a pack mentality: protect your own at all costs.

My face is the proof of scarce sleep with a bare floor against my back, sucking off my spine. Under my eyes are fat slugs, the blush of puffy eyes.

What keeps me awake in here isn't anything from out there. The only voices that rise up from outside are animal. No other sound creeps through the drafts of these old windows, except for once, maybe, just a few days after we found this place when we heard a baby crying outside. It lasted a few seconds, and might have missed our ears altogether if it hadn't gotten caught in the hairs of our arms, brushed them back until skin and follicles stood cold, puckered.

Otherwise the quiet slouches against the windows, hugs the corners of the building, but never slips through the cracks. Maybe it stays outside because it knows it isn't heavy enough to cover what's within, no competition for what we externalize, or for what's broken, disrupted under our tread.

In here, sounds spill from one room to another. Just now, a knife drops in the kitchen downstairs and the thick of its handle goes right through the walls.

And beside me every night Aimee keeps a tattooed arm over her eyes and talks in her sleep, mumbles *omission, infection, admission.*

This sprawling Victorian has its own sounds, but we aren't sure if it's the house's own spirits or things that have followed us in. Our mattresses, freed from empty houses, still hold the shape of the people who slept in them before, the shape of the dead. At night they sigh into us, spooning.

From above comes the scrape of claws. Tiny moans under the weight of the ball of a foot. Or a stiff sole, maybe.

Two girls, Brandy and Camille, went up there the other night drunk. We watched from the bottom of the stairs as Brandy's deflated mohawk and Camille's brown dreads hung like dirty tails along their backs. Climbing up, up, they giggled all the way, expecting an animal, a raccoon maybe.

"Nothing," they said when they came back down the stairs. Not giggling now, but faces full and red, nervous hands reaching to hold smoldering cigarettes. Camille hasn't come out of her room since.

And from below, agony. We never go into the basement because that's where The Shouting lives—a man's voice, but bodiless. Cam and Trevor, also drunk, went down there a few nights ago, baseball bats in hand, thinking there was perhaps an intruder down there.

"Nothing." That's what they said when they came back up, faces as plain as white t-shirts.

Later that night there was no yelling, finally. Nothing, finally. And we could have forgotten about it, probably, would have wanted to, but the boys' boots had stirred the subterranean air. It took a few days before the disruption of dust and atmosphere settled down before another shout shot up, the coarse underwing of a black bird.

This is how we live: in ancient old rooms with others like us, just as we always did. We came to this place after running into Trevor outside City Hall, lining up for rations. He remembered me and Aimee from the Mission and we remembered him from Kohl, the old goth club at Queen and Bathurst, where he used to perch on a newspaper box wearing the same torn lace top and tight black jeans every night, posing in the hopes that someone would take pity on his tentative prettiness and bring him inside for a drink.

Trevor's black dye job has grown out now, his lace top replaced with a black t-shirt, faded brown cords on his legs. We almost didn't recognize him, except that the look in his eyes is the same: part puppy, part lost boy.

But whatever collectivity we had before The End has fallen away: some here have had more primitive urges surface, creating change, clashes. Protecting what they've got, except it doesn't feel the same as when I moved in with Valium. The other girls here, Brandy and Carrie and Camille, are made of amber eyes and sharp shoulders. Me and Aimee only take our knives with us when we leave the house, but the other girls tuck blades into their boots all the time. At night they sleep between the guys, covered only by the shells of leather jackets and wiry arms. They catch me staring at their faces, trying to summon a name or a place I might have seen them at before. When our eyes meet, though, they tell me to say nothing, stay quiet, look away, so that's what I do.

You'd think no one has anything to hide anymore, but there are still pills, secret stashes, hidden connections not everyone wants to share.

This is how we live: either constantly on edge or constantly on the edge of oblivion. Some of us are like Cam, who's been on his own since his first foster home, or like Aimee, who has only ever mentioned her dead father once, her mother left unacknowledged. Myself, I spent years perfecting the art of thinking of my parents solely as a source of income and annoyance, blanking out my brother. How I live now is I don't tell anyone that my work is unraveling, that as we've stopped wondering the hows and whys of what's happening around us, today, I can't stop myself from wondering what's happening to them.

This is how we live: believing this end is a slow grind. We pick at the wet skin of lips, a miscarriage of nutrients. Eyelashes prod my tear ducts; I pluck them away and they turn to earwigs, mascara nightmares between my nails.

I will not move today. The lifeless grey meat Aimee cooked yesterday had its claws out, kept me on my knees all night. It was something Cam, our self-proclaimed hunter, had brought in, either killed on the street or found dead already. A cat, probably. There are hundreds of them out there.

Middle of the night I went outside to sweat it out, spit it up. We only have warm rainwater to drink, collected in pails on the back steps. Sand sifts at the bottom of each bucket, silt against teeth.

My mouth is raw red and vile but I can't stomach the grit of the water right now. Two more days until the next rations are handed out, if we're lucky.

I'm the only one with a sick gut. Unless the rest of them aren't showing it, better at finding privacy than I am.

This is how we live: barely, it feels. Survival strung together with the small thread of authority left in this city, no one implementing rules because there's nothing to save, and not enough of a population to police. We expect every care package to be our last, don't even ask questions when we pick it up, just take what we can, add it all to our small stockpiles of salvaged batteries, scavenged items looted from hollowed out convenience stores, the rubbing alcohol and antiseptic creams we've taken from abandoned houses.

Aimee's up, her body a pink silhouette in the corner of my eye. She says something but the bedroom's too hot for me to even breathe in so I move to the bathroom without answering her, press myself against the bare tub, seeking a cool surface.

Someone's hung up shower curtains, cloudy clear plastic with black polka dots. Optimism, maybe, that we'll be able to squeeze a shower or two out of the taps one of these days. You never know. The grid seems to flicker on and off, out of nowhere. Anything can happen.

There's a clanging of metal from the mudroom at the back of the house, blending with the chainsaw of runny lungs. Must be Cam or Trevor, who are constantly bringing back things they find in the streets, along with illnesses. Sickness is always running through this house, runs through the city still.

"Bikes."

It's the only word I can hear through the bathroom floor. The guys raise their pitch when they say it, excited. They've been picking them up all over the place, they said. Just cutting the locks and taking them. Not likely that anyone will come looking for them.

From downstairs, Aimee's maple voice asks: "Where we gonna ride them to?" My head is swimming too much to tap into recognition patterns. Another wave of cramps passes through my abdomen and I don't hear the answer, just close my eyes. Hope to sleep past the pain.

A few hours of half-sleep and the space where the ache was has been filled with what I hope are slivers of hunger. Downstairs, Cam's showing off a find of thirty boxes of packaged cakes and donuts looted from the waste bin behind a warehouse west of downtown they found when they went out riding earlier. The boxes are all marked expired but the cakes are still soft in their sealed plastic, no mold. Good enough. Better than the dried beans and maggoty rice in the kitchen.

All afternoon, the crush and snap of plastic wrapping torn open runs parallel to the tears in every roll of my stomach. I can only eat a bite of vanilla, something soft and bland enough to keep down.

8

A SÉANCE OF WHITE NOISE

The electricity weaves us with black and white. Cuts in and out, unpredictable but enough to let us have something, to give us what we really need.

We all ride together from the Victorian, pull up outside the charred shell of what used to be the Mission, a pack of clanging chains and steel toe tension, thin red bandanas tied to pale ankles. The marquee has held on, hangs empty, but we don't need it to tell us why we're here. We have messages written on windows, word of mouth, longing and intuition. There aren't as many people outside as I was expecting. The building is hollowed out, becoming an unholy structure, its ceiling blasted by flames.

Cam says he heard the band's worried that they might not get through their whole set, not sure how much electricity there is. It could all be blown out by their amps.

Someone wonders out loud if this is the best idea, if we should save the energy for something else. Everyone groans, throws stony faces towards the question. What else is there if we can't have one more show? Besides, Cam points out, the power cuts in and out anyway. No one's got a rein on it no matter what you use it for.

Me and Aimee stare hard at the few kids out here: a girl with silver eyes and a face so freckled it looks tan. Her mouth is small and hard and the spiked dog collar around her neck is too loose. The two guys she's with could be the same person: shaved heads, complexion made of paste. I don't know any of them. If they know we're checking them out they don't act like it. Don't even look at us. They adjust their weight every few seconds. Dusty plastic capsules crunch under their heels. The sound of snail shells.

Grayline. Another mumble from Cam. Keeping his voice low, he tells us that people want to know how to get it, what it is. The story is that grayline's a drug made from the shake of magic mushrooms and the ashes of the dead. That crematoriums have been pillaged to make it. Cam adds cryptically, "I know where to get some."

Me and Aimee used to know where to get everything but now we're behind, relying on Cam more than we'd like to. Unlike Trevor's, Cam's eyes hold a hardness that betrays any softening expressions in his face. Aimee says one of her half-brothers knew Cam for a while, that he had a reputation for paranoia and the ability to go from calm to vicious with nothing more than a glance from across the room. Twice now I've heard Cam talk about how he spent his sixteenth birthday in jail for beating the crap out of another kid for reasons that are only ever vaguely explained.

We hover around him anyway, waiting on his word.

"Can you tell us where?" Aimee asks, but Cam just shakes his head, enjoying this power he has. Instead of saying anything, he unrolls his fist and holds three capsules up, one for each of us. We break them open, pour the grayline on our tongues like Cam shows us, and wait for the show to start.

Aimee offers the last drag of her cigarette. Another thing that probably won't last much longer. Every pack we've been given has been stale. Probably old smokes that were sitting around in some warehouse for years. No point in complaining. Soon we'll forget what fresh cigarettes taste like. I kill the smoke, drop it, put it out with the toe of my boot. A green sticker in the shape of a star is stuck to the sidewalk. One of its glittering points is peeling upwards, reaching for sky.

Inside Cam disappears and Trevor comes up to us right away, his hair in his eyes and his face too close to mine. The toes of his shoes jam into the front of my boots. He holds his hand up to us the way people offer food to an animal.

He asks if we want some more. I look to Aimee to answer but she's already reaching in, helping herself, so I do the same, not mentioning that I can already feel Cam's dose working through me.

"Thanks," we say, cracking the plastic caps open and pouring the contents onto our tongues. In our mouths, it cakes into a dry dust, doesn't work itself into paste but instead goes down like grit. Saliva glands pump liquid but it only spreads the granules high up into my gums.

This must be what death tastes like. Trevor just nods, watches us work it all down our throats as he brushes hair back from his forehead with his whole hand. Trevor's t-shirt is slit below the armpit, thin cotton fighting long underarm hairs.

Grayline. I would have thought it was just sand if it wasn't for the physical click, distinct and muscular, a strobe light through my arms and legs. Across the room a couple of people are putting up missing persons posters: friends and parents, a couple of cousins. The words are written in red nail polish, faded marker, black electrical tape. I wonder how many posters it took before the ink ran out of those people's pens.

Each rectangle that gets stuck to the wall throbs out towards me as I pass by, puffing out paper bellies to show me their secrets, hidden messages spelling out the night's song list, translating into bending steel strings, margins blotting into fret boards.

White Doom aren't going on for another hour but I can already feel them, hear them. They're pulling me in, tentacles of reverb wrapped around nerves, sucking my hangnails, scraping circles around my gooseflesh. Another poster throbs into a bass line, water witching with the majority of flesh, my liquid foundation.

Aimee is stealing my breath with every word she's saying, the word thirteen coming out of her mouth so many times that it's growing into $13+13=26+13=39+13=52+13=65$ and on and on.

The Mission is hundreds of feet of black gravity, too deep for the eyes to adjust. I light a match, but burn the tips of my thumb and finger one step later. When I get back into the light I will see that it's left a dark brown bubble of sulfur and body water on my skin.

White Doom take the stage surrounded by small bodies. I am thirty seconds behind everybody else, having now created my own time. The band did not start on my schedule. They open with "Omen/coincidence." The first bars don't come *from* the band, but instead come *to* the band through us, our bodies mere vessels so that this one night might happen, the light of the low stars a gift we draw from to power these instruments and fingers and voices, not a song but a reversal of ruin that brings us back from the dead, gives us witch-name initials and brands them into our retinas.

We form a triple circle, guided by subconscious subversions, natural rhythms and the shadow hands of conjured spectres, a primary sacrament with our hands cupped into scrying bowls. A girl falls and her dive breaks the inner circle, making her an altar of truth. We all follow.

White Doom spiral into "White Cat" but I must be in a trance, must actually be inside the songs instead of in front of them, because when you get inside there is no distinguishing one song from the next. This band is reducing us all to a single consciousness, a new collective consciousness, and right now I do believe that this is the culmination of everything we've been dying for, that this moment is the whole point of The End and everyone here, that we are the lucky ones, the ones that are crossing over.

A boy with neon nail polish grabs the tops of my arms. His hands are made of babies' bones and wrapped in skin as thin as tissue paper. He pulls me down with him to pray: *I need you I need you I need you.* He must have seen that I'm the one here who really understands those words.

But then another voice overrides his and puts communion into my head, just as cascades of feedback spill onto the floor around us. The band sits on the floor, too, staring down, waiting for the right time to kick the fuzz into a semblance of a song. A few girls sit on the band's amps, arms around each other, their faces beacons of adoration. *This is all we have.*

All we ever had, I answer.

9

COMEDOWN

Watching dregs of web in the tub, waiting for the grayline comedown to kick in. Cam didn't mention this shit would last so long.

The spiders work over the taps, all the way up to the dank angle where the walls turn into ceiling. Pretend the wet crawl of spider spit isn't what it is. Pretend it's a frail line of bubble bath. Channel decadence. Bathe in collected rainwater. Hope that body heat will be enough to warm it up. Pretend the soap didn't come from a care package, something cheap and practical and unscented. Ignore the tightening skin, the flakes it leaves in your hair.

Think back to when Aimee was living on Manning, the clawfoot bathtub on the day I got evicted. Spent an hour in pink heat, perfumed water bubbling with the scent of roses while Aimee sliced watermelon in the kitchen, left it waiting for me until I came out of the bathroom, wrapped in the cool silk of her robe. Channel decadence.

Aimee's got her period. While I'm in the tub she's washing out her homemade pads in the sink beside me. The only girl here who still gets a period. The rest of us are simply too emaciated. Aimee's just as underfed but somehow her body hangs on.

A guy showed up here after the White Doom show, wasted and saying he'd "eat out any girl on her rag," convinced women pass on their proteins through menstrual blood. "All I want to do is lick at girls who've got blood coming out of their crotches," he said, adding that he'd trade it for a mickey of rye. Aimee was the only one who took advantage of the offer, but the others tried: Brandy offered a bony ass, Carrie the light brush of the wide space between her thighs.

Me and Aimee didn't talk about it after because we knew this water could never get you clean enough. No point in spreading the mess around.

Channel decadence.

Don't hesitate, just go.

Anticipating the dread but it doesn't come. There's too much dampness for it to cut through. There are no more days where you leave your jacket open at the end of winter to feel the freedom of a warmer spring wind snaking down the arms, up the back. There are no more days when your legs ache from struggling against newly packed snow. Now, when it's not sticky hot there's a biting dampness, something that comes in too close.

Trevor's heard about a coffee shop open on the west side of Queen Street that sells coffee in exchange for whatever you could offer: a cup of rice, a roll of gauze, a needle and thread.

"I heard the guy running it will take a hug and a kiss as payment, if you're a girl," Trevor says.

Me and Aimee decide to check it out. Aside from a barter system we don't know how they're holding it together and don't really want to. In seconds we go from being curious to needy, hungering to taste something real, to ease through the comedown we knew would be on us at any moment.

We ask Trevor if he wants to come but he shakes his head, no. "Me and Cam are patrolling again today," he says.

Me and Aimee roll our eyes at the word "patrolling," which is what Cam calls walking around, looking to see what's still out there. They map out dead landmarks and squats on the living room wall, write down the addresses of houses they've broken into. They've yet to come back emptyhanded. A couple days ago it was a case of cat food. Another, two pearl necklaces, which Trevor gave to me and Aimee when Cam wasn't looking.

Aimee moves to a row of sharpened sticks lined up in the mudroom and chooses two, holds one out to me, I slide it into my backpack. We all help make spears, to keep the dogs away. I haven't had to use one yet and I don't know if I could drive it in hard enough if I had to. We bring a pocket comb and a bar of soap and hope it will be enough to buy us something warm and wakening at the coffee shop.

On bikes, we coast around stalled cars and pump our legs up every incline. Our bodies are getting hard. We are turning to stone, though, not strength. Our thighs fight with us to preserve nutrients, to hang onto every calorie just to stay awake. Since the fires and the suck of sound, since the disappearances and the dead weather, the city seemed to expand, its streets lengthened for miles with blanks inserted where structure and density used to be.

We pass the park where Hunter and I once fell asleep under a tree on a summer night, drunk and giving in easily to circumstance, spontaneity. Today there's a dead body, right where we'd drifted off, clothes and limbs torn near clean. Death by dog, it seems.

The coffee shop has no sign, but it's marked by the heavy condensation in the front window, beads of water streaking down. Something clawing its way out. Two feet from the door is a fecal smear, watery and voluminous. We're starting to recognize the angles and shapes of shit, can tell whether it's human or animal. This one is definitely human. Inside, the place is packed, but there are only twenty seats. The tables are small, chairs so close together everyone is almost touching. Everyone's looking at each other, wondering where we all came from. There's no sense of relief at seeing others, no effort to come together. There is a table between four men. Aimee tells me to hold it while she orders. To my left a man snorts inwards, hard, sucking back snot. I can hear him swallow it. I swallow too, fighting a lump of rising nausea. I can't tell if this is part of the grayline comedown or just everyday disgust.

I hold my breath, waiting for his cough to come but it doesn't. I have to breathe. The relief in a held breath is not in new oxygen but in letting go of the pain of what's trapped inside.

Behind the counter is a man whose muscles have gone soft but still show the bulk his body once held. His eyes are half-hidden with heavy brows, grey cats' tails to match that of the feline now prowling between people's legs under the shop's tables.

Aimee makes her order and smiles, but the man just nods, says nothing as he turns to fill our cups. He nods again as he takes the comb and soap, wordlessly sliding them under the counter. His left arm is pitted with a dog bite, two perfect rows of scabbed red holes. It reminds me of something I heard once: that if a dog's tasted blood, he can never be the same again, that the hot copper touch on his tongue takes away the taste for anything else. We should have brought him one of our spears.

Aimee sets down our drinks, black coffee in black mugs dark enough to hide the dirt, old imprints of other people's lips. We don't ask how anything is washed, or where the water for the coffee came from. Don't care anyway. Caffeine is a buzz that's been missing from our bloodstreams for so long that we just want to get it into us.

A film of phlegm breaks from someone's throat in the back corner. Aimee turns, instinctively. Personal space is always shifting in the old Victorian, never knowing who's going to show up, but we are never this close together, never nearly shoulder to shoulder with so many strangers. The crowd, it's more than we expected. Hadn't thought this far ahead about how we would handle the claustrophobia. My throat digs up a tickle already, hint of a sting. Despite the charcoal weather outside it's too hot in here. Aimee's hair is curling at her temples. She holds it off her neck with one hand. I keep my sweater on, feel safer in its husk even though it could drown me right now.

The coffee is hot. We blow the steam from its surface. I imagine the top of my mug is already skating with viruses, germs in the air. I imagine them being lifted off with every puff, or killed by the heat of the water. The man beside me finally lets a cough loose, holds a handkerchief to his mouth to spit. I keep the mug to my lips, breathe in the steam instead of the impurity from the table next to me.

A table shifts upwards. People are getting ready to leave. Someone bumps into Aimee's chair. She turns, glares, but they're already on their way out and don't say anything.

I notice then that we're the only women in here. The other girls in our house, for all their hardened edges, won't leave without one of the guys with them, not even in a group. We still don't know all that's out there yet, but we do know there's more empty space than ever, the least amount of witnesses around.

I wonder if Aimee's noticed that we're only among men. Neither of us is saying much, senses too aware of every sound and smell. Setting us on edge. Talk and we could be under threat if we give in to distraction, give in to relaxation. I feel dizzy by the time I'm halfway through my coffee. Aimee, too, light-headed and almost done. We chug. The hot water burns, reverse acid reflux. It brings on another lump of nausea and I don't want to regret that last hard swallow. It might be the last coffee of my life. Standing, my head fades from grey to black to grey again in a head rush as I push my way out from behind the table, following Aimee back outside. With shaking hands, we do up our jackets for the ride back to the house.

Halfway there it starts to snow, frenetic temperature dropping all around us, cold pressing through, clawing beneath our t-shirts. The light's dropping, too, sun fading fast even though it feels like it's only been up for a few hours.

Or maybe *we've* only been up for a few hours.

Aimee pulls out ahead of me and wipes out seconds later, tires slipping in the snow. We decide to walk the bikes the rest of the way. Over the Bloor Street bridge the streetlights are rolling on and off, waves of malfunction and shadow as the daylight fades. The snow that lands now dries in heaps like piles of salt, crunches under our steps. With the orange lights dipping us in and out of the dark it's hard tell what's puke and what's snow, everything showing up like pale chunks in the night. I'm not clear-headed enough to see where I'm stepping anyway.

Aimee tells me a story. "My friend contacted a ghost through a Ouija board once. The ghost told her if she ever wanted to see him, all she had to do was look at the streetlights. After that, every light she'd walk under would flicker. He was always there."

The snow has stopped by the time we get to the top of our street, but the night's still damp. Traces of grayline are still sending small shocks through me, lightning residuals bruising me from the inside. The comedown overrides the caffeine, and the exhaustion I feel coming on is deadening. We get inside and I crawl up the stairs and onto my mattress, so tired that for the first time since we got here I am something close to comfortable.

- 10 -
PATTERNS

One of the girls has gone missing. "She was right there/I just saw her/she was right there/I just saw her." This is what I hear before even get up. Brandy and Carrie take it up as a chant. This is how I know what happened before seeing the vacant space where Camille used to sleep.

Gone. Disappeared like so many others already have. We didn't know this was still happening to people, that it could still happen to people. We still don't know where people disappear to.

I didn't really know her, other than the incongruity of her lilies-and-lace name against her brown dreads, stained wife beater, bare feet, black cargo shorts. Not that any of us could be so delicate now, even if we wanted to. She'd kept away from us, hiding from whatever ghosts she'd seen upstairs. "She just wants to be alone," Brandy had told us whenever we'd asked. I wonder if she's alone where she is now.

Question: How do you adjust to a near-empty city?

1. You don't. Your thought patterns are too routed. You find, surprisingly, that your relationships with the streets are defined by your relationships with the people you shared those streets with, even if only in passing. You step out onto what used to be the city's busiest sidewalks and you catch yourself thinking, "It's so quiet this morning," and then you remember why, as if any day now this will all go back to normal.

2. You don't know who is still around and who isn't. You don't know whether houses are empty or occupied. You watch for a twitch of a curtain, a face at the window. You listen for hysteria calling out from behind closed doors.

3. You don't know if you want people to still be around or not. You don't know if you're better off being one of the last, because you can't gauge the alternative. Whoever's still around could be dangerous. But they could also be someone you want, or need.

4. You don't know if the people who've disappeared are happy or dead, or happier dead. You don't know if maybe they knew something you didn't. Can't help but wonder if everyone escaped, all went somewhere safe, somewhere better, and you somehow missed out.

Maybe you're not a survivor at all, but just another one of the dead who doesn't know it's time to stop breathing.

Trevor pins me up against the wall and breathes into my nose.

"Can you smell anything?" he asks.

I turn my head to breathe out the shit-stink of dry mouth and decaying food he's just plastered across my face.

"Smell what?" I ask.

"Dick. Do I smell like dick? I sucked some guy for this." Trevor holds up a one-litre bottle of wine, an animal proud to bring home its kill.

"No, you're fine," I tell him.

"Good," he says. "Don't tell Cam, k? I'm going to say I traded for it, if he asks."

"Why?"

"I want him to think I'm something else," Trevor says. "Something tougher. Cam says it's weak, to give away sex for something you want."

"Okay," I say. "I won't tell him."

Later, we sit in a circle on the floor and pass the bottle around. The wine burns an empty stomach, digestion contracting around its crimson acidity.

Aimee: You want to know about my parents? No, sorry. I don't talk about that.

Cam: The first time my dad went to jail he was twenty-one. He went in for burglary and assault. Later he went back for possession, burglary again, and grand theft. He always told me he regretted it—especially the assault—but also said that what he'd done had made sense at the time. When I was little—this was way before I went to a foster home—I remember he'd said a couple times, "You won't do what I've done, will you?" And I'd shake my head, no, and he'd say, "No, I know you won't, because you're better than me."

After I went to jail nothing was really the same between us. Because for one, I was five years younger than he was when he first got arrested, and two, I think he really believed I was a different person than I ended up becoming.

Brandy: What happened to him?

Cam: Heart attack. Last year. He was out at a bar with his girlfriend and some guy tried to hit on her or something and they got into it. The fight got broken up pretty quick but I guess my dad was really wound up about it. They went home a couple hours later and that's when he started having chest pain. Apparently he collapsed just as the ambulance was called—boom! Dead, just like that.

I don't know where my mom got to. She didn't even come to the funeral, so . . .

Carrie: Wow, shitty.

Trevor: My dad hated me because he thought I was—and I quote—"a fag." I never wanted to be home so I started staying out all the time. I even lived at Kohl for a while. They had these great booths you could fit right under and hide while they locked up for the night. I also slept in the coat check room for four weeks before I got caught.

I thought they were gonna call the cops, or at least kick me out for sure, but I got lucky. They asked me what I was doing and when I told them, the bartender said she'd gone through the same thing with her parents and invited me to stay on her couch until I could figure something out.

Brandy: I'm from up north. I came here on a bus when I was eighteen. I didn't hate my parents, just the place I grew up in.

Trevor: Do you think your parents are still alive?

Brandy: Yeah, I do actually. I can't explain it, but I think of them and I can feel them there. Do you know what I mean?

I'm going to get up there. I don't know how yet. Maybe I'll just start walking one day.

Cam: Or you could take a bike. How long would walking take?

Brandy: Days. But I've got the time.

Carrie: I'm from B.C. I'll never get home from here. It's weird, though. I'd wanted to leave for so long and when I finally did, I never thought I'd want to go back.

Ang: My parents treated me differently. After I tried to kill myself, you know? I lived with them for a while, after it happened, and they only ever talked to me in questions: "How are you today? Would you like this? Is it okay if we do this? Is it okay if I move this here? Is the volume of the TV bothering you? Is it too sunny for you to sit outside?"

I thought it would be different when I moved out again, but it wasn't. "When can we see you?" I felt like they always wanted me to come over just to make sure I was alive. They didn't actually want to talk to me, or know me anymore, because they didn't know what to do with someone who'd come back from the dead.

A groan rises from the basement, its tone sharpening to a point. It feels too early to hear so much phantom agony. Something about the shouting makes me think: Dad. Which makes me think: Mom. Which makes me think: Go, today.

Today? I'm not ready to know the answers to the questions I'm afraid to even fully form yet but tell myself, yes, today.

But only after a little more sleep. It will take at least an hour to ride to my old house, and how fast I'll need to move all depends on what I run into when I'm out there.

Her palm is a blunt slam into my cheekbone. It lands more like a shove than a slap, probably because there's no meat left in my face.

Above me, she's a flash of blue hair and orange lipstick, knees on either side of me in an expert straddle that didn't even wake me up.

"You!" she says. "I. Know. You." She digs a finger deep into my sternum when she says the second *you*, like it's an accusation.

There's a sweetheart bruise on the inside of her thigh, like she's been rubbing against a pole for the last six months.

"I know you, too," I say.

Tara. I remember her being to the left of the stage, at any Valium show within a five-hour radius of her hometown. She'd followed us to a few after-parties but never said much, just that she worked as a dancer. Instead of talking she mostly smoked furiously and stared, as if she was waiting for someone to see her.

Tara's from a time when the Valium fans in her town used to go down to the graveyard. They had their own sect, their own rites, one of which was built out of an annual Devil's night summoning. It had once just meant getting drunk and stoned and a little scared, but that particular night it would be sacred.

At least they'd hoped, never really expected what actually happened: the graves opening up, swallowing them whole. The rest of the town thought it was a mass suicide, another sign that The End was upon us.

"I don't know where I was during that time, or how long I was gone," she says, still hovering over me. "I just know that in a dream I was told that, to be reborn, I'd have to become hard enough to claw through a door that gaped like a mouth."

Tara's spent the last three weeks sleeping in a backyard shed.

"There were still bodies in the house," she says. "You could smell them from the back steps."

She was walking by and saw Cam and Trevor outside, sharpening knives. "They said you just had a bed free up," Tara says. "I didn't know *you'd* be here, though."

My hair's grown out, long dark roots even darker against the flash of peroxide. I wonder if anyone else from my past life will still be around to recognize me.

"Have you ever forgotten what you were before?" she asks. "Have you ever lost your history?"

I want to tell her yes, that there've been times when all I had left were the bags under my eyes. But her eyes are oceans, and it's through those waters I know she's lost her original voice. I hear it through the undertow.

"Have you ever tried to find yourself in someone's lap, Ang? Or gotten so wasted that all you could do was wait for the floor to fall away?"

Something like seeing the future in her face, her posture. The way the light falls over the gouges where her eyes have started to sink in. You can tell what she'd look like if she could get older: body hard with old pride, everything lined and heavily used.

Tara punches the mattress, grazes my ear. "*What* are you doing here, Ang?" she asks, a rush of blood daring to fill her cheeks. "Do you know how much I believed you? Do you know what you've made me question?"

I don't, no, but I can't bring myself to tell her this. I should be at my parents' house. I shouldn't have stayed in bed.

"You promised to die, Ang," Tara says. "You were part of something that you couldn't honour. And even now, when everything has turned to shit, you stay."

She climbs off me and I barely feel a shift from her weight. She slings her bag over her shoulder but she only takes two steps towards the door before whipping around.

"You owe me, Ang. You owe me an answer, at least."

- 11 -
WHAT WE COULD HAVE HAD

The doors are locked when I get there and the windows are still intact. I can't let myself take it as a sign that anyone's home, though, so I distract myself with other possibilities: were the suburbs completely wiped out, even of looters? Or is everything here still so sleepy that no one's even noticed what's happening around them?

But no, these streets can't be untouched. There are too many locked-out cats darting under dry bushes, too much grass turned golden. And the silence here is just as deep as downtown, like a hand covering an open mouth to stifle a scream.

The spare key is still dangling from a wind chime on the back deck. I brace for death stench to hit me but all I get when I walk in is air gone stagnant. I know the house is empty, can feel it before I even call out. There's something about the bearing of the walls, as if they've exhaled and forgot to start breathing again.

"Hello?" I say, but it comes out quieter than I want it to. "Mom?"

There's a tremor in the word. I don't have control over my voice in here. But then I never did.

Upstairs, the beds are made. My old room turned guest bedroom, untouched. My parents' bed, perfect, as if they'd gotten up, like usual, on their last day, as if they'd assumed it would end just like every other day. On their nightstand, a photograph of the four of us, me and my brother in the middle. I lean across the bed for it and find the pillows have held onto the oils of my parents' hair. I pull both of them to me, bury myself.

Instead of them, though, I think of Hunter—what we knew of each other, what we had trusted. Our connection was held together by morbidity and attraction. There must have been more to it than that but you know, it's getting hard for me to remember. Not because I can't recall it but because I don't know that I want to.

Hunter, the details of your face, even, I sometimes think about letting them slip away. I am slipping away. I had a dream you were here. Outside on the street. With you was a dog, big but friendly. Somehow you'd found me. We considered it magic, ESP. You let your dog do the talking. It licked my hair, licked the shine and dirt off my face. Its tongue was very, very soft.

Hunter, would we have been happy? Would we have been happy if we had made different decisions? If we'd chosen life instead?

Would we have had a house like this one someday, Hunter? Would we have had comfort and routine? I wasn't ready for what happened the day of our pact. I wasn't ready for the rest of my life.

Did it happen to you, too? Did you feel the same fear I did? Death took you over so fast, I never got to ask. Maybe you were strong enough to push through it. Did I give in to weakness, cave to hesitation too soon? Did my adrenaline convince me to fight for a life I'd never wanted? Even now, I don't have the energy or confidence to fight my body's craving for life. Even now, still, I don't have the energy to fight my cowardice at calling 911 as soon as your eyes closed.

I will not go to my brother's basement bedroom. Instead, I fill my bag with my mom's underwear, my dad's socks. The drawers are lined with tiny hotel soaps, something my mom used to do to keep things scented. I take them all.

There's a stash of matches in a shoebox at the bottom of the closet, souvenirs from bars and hotels they'd visited, most from a time before I was born. I poke through my mom's jewelry but only take one thing, a gold necklace with a heart-shaped locket, a gift I'd picked out with my dad for her birthday when I was in Grade 5. She'd left the locket empty. I breathe into it, make a wish.

The kitchen cupboards are full of pots and pans but little food: a half-eaten box of saltines, salt and pepper, two cans of soup. I take it all. Then I lock up and take the spare key, too.

- 12 -
A BEAUTIFUL CORPSE

Shit Kitten is playing in an old brick factory at the edge of an urban forest. All I want is to get there, but Tara wants to do complicated things and won't let me leave.

She suggests the choking game. Believes I can handle it because although she's lost some of her history she knows mine immediately, knows what I've done and where it led. But I don't have enough breath left to apply pressure to a throat. Tara just answers with a kiss thick with deep throat saliva, something that tastes like an old push for survival. In her grip I am dust on a lens. Eyes open but unclear. She knows I only pretend to half-remember my past.

Tara says her memory is like an awkward grind, forever up against the rough fabric of a crotch, riding a sticky lap. Beyond that admission she says nothing.

"Okay," I say. "You're right. I'm sorry."

We can see into each other, both having been halfway to the other side. Her eyes sparkle with the moment before a kiss. Mine, shocked with the insecurity they surrender. I knot that nervous energy in a pack of hair, hang it in a window. Hope its light reaches me.

Tara casts a darkening crown upon herself as she pulls the blue wig over her head. Along with it comes the smell of sweat embedded in the nylon hairline. She's encased in torn silk and black lace. She wears no bra and the nubs that were her breasts peek through the top of her thin camisole like a hot implication.

She keeps her last tube of burnt orange lipstick sitting tight in the pocket of her black leather shorts. When she leans into the corner of the cracked mirror to colour her lips there's enough of a wink from the tops of her thighs to know she's not wearing underwear.

Her lipstick is down to a nub. It seeps at her mouth. There's no more makeup to buy, it being one of the first things that ran out, one of the first things we noticed was missing off the store shelves. Not enough of a necessity over batteries and lighter fluid and dried foods, even though everyone still wanted to paint their faces. We've held on to whatever we could: dried up compacts, flaking palettes, lipsticks down to their final strokes.

In our dreams we have everything. In our hands we hold the things we really want and believe them to be ours. It's not until we start to wake up that we remember dream objects can't travel back to the waking world. We don't get to keep them. The only way we can get them again is to stay asleep and we try, but that sleep won't stay on us.

I sit on the floor beside Tara, squeeze my face into a slit of glass, smoke a stub of eyeliner across my lids, smudge it with cigarette ash to make it stretch. The glass of the mirror is tinged with yellow; it reflects the room back three shades darker, makes us look even more tired than we are. Tara's face takes over the mirror, shoving me out.

"I used to watch you, you know," she says. "You and the other Valium girls. Some of my friends wanted to make up a name for all of you. The Valleys or something. Ha! That would've been pretty stupid. Well some of the other girls thought you were pretty stupid. I'd hear them in the bathroom, talking. They were waiting for any of you to fuck it up, make the wrong move and kill your relationships. It was all jealousy, though. Everyone knew you were the most beautiful girls. You had the best style. Everyone wanted to be you, but that made it hard to like you, you know? Because you had this thing we all wanted. The scene itself could have felt like a family, but you were part of this inner circle that some people thought was hard to become a part of. It was almost like you were on the outside for a lot of us, even though you were in the center of everything."

Tara talks at me through the mirror. It slants her face, brings one eye higher than the other.

"I heard Hunter wasn't always nice to everyone," she says, "but he was nice to me."

Tara turns to me now, with her face back on straight. We both nod, an unspoken understanding that we are each other's reluctant links to the past.

Shit Kitten's playing tonight, running on generators or finding a bump in the thin power grid. We don't care how the music happens just so long as it does, so long as their sound can still slam through bodies so our bodies can slam together.

The building's old and full of stone, properly absorbent, abandoned years before we ever found it. People used to have parties here. I heard, a long time ago, that a girl fell off the catwalk one time and died. That was years back, though. Nobody could come around for months after. The cops kept it guarded, warned people away.

If any of us die tonight, no one will ever know. I like this privacy, fold it into the palm of my hand as we take a shortcut through the trees, down the hill, knives and sticks pointed, ready for anything. Around us the forest is a backdrop of kindling—bare trees rubbing their branches together—eager trembling hands.

Instead of an opening band there's a ritual chanted out by a thin girl in a long, loose-knit sweater; its collar looped around her shoulders, runs in the fabric zigzagging all the way down her arms. The sleeves bunch at her wrists, cover her hands. She doesn't wear pants, only black underwear and motorcycle boots. Her lips are stretched, like they don't fit her face. She keeps her mouth on the microphone as a high, honeyed chant rises up from below her navel.

The girl arcs her neck as a guttural moan shakes through her, forces her head back so we can see there's a second set of teeth growing from the roof of her mouth, each ending in fine points. Beside her is a guy, hair blonde and long enough to touch his waist. He's shirtless: on his chest shines a scar, fresh. As people file past, some of them touch the raised tissue, pause to fully flatten their palms over the inverted star carved there.

There is nothing but noise building behind them, a beaten up synthesizer pushing out a tantalizing wave of fuzz tinged with migraine—just enough to keep us cuddled in a cold canopy of sound. The girl's voice has risen again and the guy joins her, his vocal chords stretching to reach hers until they sound identical, interchangeable.

Someone has made a bar out of milk crates and cinder blocks. Tara comes away with plastic cups in each hand, deep purple liquid streaking the backs of her hands.

"Tooth found a shitload of Kool-Aid, apparently," she says, handing me a cup of homemade vodka with a splash of grape. It's been so long since I've had a drink with this much sugar, even this small amount. Granules of sweet crunch against my teeth. I know I'll have a headache tomorrow but right now all I want is the extra few beats the vodka is kicking into my heart.

Aimee's moved off into the crowd and Tara's turning to me to talk, touching me with every other word tonight. "Things find you," she says, and I don't know if she's talking about me or about herself or about this place. Whichever it is, she's right, and as the vodka hits the back of my neck with a rush of warmth I know there is nothing else we need to say.

Cam's hair is getting long, keeps getting in his eyes. It's how I recognize him coming up behind Tara. He won't take his hand off of her to brush the strands away. Tara's hand glides over his eyebrow, tucks an angled tuft behind his right ear.

"Thanks," he says, smiling without looking at me.

He and Tara act like they slept together once, like they would do it again the way he's distracted by the curve of her waist, his fingers pumping to underline a point. My eyes are on his collarbone; a chin could fit there, nose slipping under his jaw, eyelashes tickling the back of his ear. A shiver could pass between him and a girl then, if he'd let anyone be so close.

"You excited?" Tara asks him.

"Of course," Cam says. "I was made for these times."

I roll my eyes. Cam doesn't know what it's like to live through a lost identity. He hasn't yet accepted that there will be no news stories about all this, no books in the aftermath, praising us survivors as heroes. There will be no after at all.

Tara's left hand pecks nervously at her right, pulls at a hang-nail on her middle finger. She's slipped her boots off to wrap and unwrap her toes around her Achilles tendons. She sees someone she thinks is familiar, opens her mouth as he walks by but it's a false memory. She tells me she thought it was a guy she might have almost slept with this one time—kind of nice, kind of smart, but boring. "Boring boring boring," she says, "an automatic write-off." They got as close as forehead to forehead, staring and smiling at each other in pre-kiss state. Except his head had an extra layer of fat, enough padding that it felt like she was leaning her head against the heel of a hand instead of the smooth bone of a skull. "Still," she says, "if it was now, I'd sleep with him, consid-ering the circumstances."

Shit Kitten is three songs into its set. We stay sitting because this is where we feel the music the most, conducted through the floor. Aimee finds us, sits, too, because this how it gets into you, beats the shit out of you. It comes crawling up from the earth and simultaneously dives right into your heart head-on, hits your chest from top and bottom, fists a cardiac hole and then fucks your aorta, ventricles, pummels your blood. By the speaker is where the abuse happens, where you give yourself up for this, give yourself over to the music, to the music's mind.

There's a tail coiled in my left side, burning above my pubic bone. It twitches, like an animal dreaming.

Aimee asks, "You feeling okay?"

The tip of the tail tickles my stomach into a slow flip. Tara offers me a drink from her cup. I shake my head, keep my mouth closed. Not that it really matters what goes in, what comes out, where it lands. Rattail used to keep a bucket in front of his mic stand for when he had to puke. His blood was made mostly of a mix of speed and mushrooms, alcohol and a dab of heroin that he said he used "here and there." In Shit Kitten's early days he said it was nerves, that he had to get so fucked up just to sing, his stom-ach knotting up under the crunch of his abdomen, the strain on his vocal chords pushing down so hard that he just couldn't keep anything down. But we never really believed that. He had too much confidence for it to be nerves, and if you were ever hanging out with the band before or after, you probably saw Rattail's eyes roll all the way up into his head, so far in fact that whole minutes would pass by before you saw him come back again, a testament to just how wasted he could get.

Another song in and my nausea passes, the belly-deep tail settling enough for another splash of purple and vodka. Someone's passing around grayline and my dose collects in a chemical drip at the back of my throat; I can feel the slow pull every time I swallow.

Rattail's crawling through the next song, almost crying through the words. There is no stage, just a circle of dirt where the concrete floor ends.

The back of Rattail's t-shirt is shredding, mostly hanging off his chest, front-heavy. He flops onto his side, a tired dog, and whimpers out a few lines. People around us are electric, with so much heat running between them that it's melted the soles of their shoes to the floor. Their bodies collide but never move from their places.

Rattail's voice might have gone from aluminum thunder to a serrated lullaby but the guitars are still at full roar, still have us in their jaws. Cam's in front of us, on his knees in the dirt, listening for the quietest words. He's holding his hair back now, face serious, concentrating on the messages in the music; his knuckles huge and almost black they're so dirty, an eye drawn on the back of his hand, watching.

I can't tell if Shit Kitten's still playing the same song or if they've moved on. It's all a swirl of destroyed sound now, revving distortion, a razorblade grazing a thin black stocking.

Rattail's not moving anymore, hasn't sang or even whispered a note in I don't know how long. Feels like it's been at least an hour but Cam's inked eye is still staring, unblinking, from the back of his hand. He's still crouched there, same position. No one could stay like that for so long, could they?

Cam always says drugs slow your time down because they bring you closer to death, and the closer to death you are the slower everything gets. Time only accelerates when you are at your most alive. By that logic we'll be dead any minute now.

The guitars do stop, finally, fade out and disappear like a screen gone to black. The tail's slipped out of my stomach to twist through the crowd, a purple trail chasing loose hems. Outside, someone's gotten a fire going. The heat is bright enough to bathe us. It crisps the skin of my face, makes me feel the cleanest I've been in weeks.

A thick fog hangs low over the trees, three-quarters of the way over their peaks. If we weren't all in t-shirts you could believe it was almost close to something like cold out here. A semicircle of people crowd around the fire. The chanting girl that opened is there, too, sitting on a dented folding chair. I don't recognize her until the tip of her cigarette lights up her face. Her leather boots are rotted through across the tops where her toes bend, the heels worn into upward curves. The intake of smoke from her cigarette sparks an orange puff of light across the bottom half of her face. At the corner of her eye, crisscrossing up to her temple is a dark sparkle, a charcoal swirl.

"I can paint your face, too," she says. That's when I notice she doesn't blink, that her eyes are only white with black, the eyes of something that once lived in deep water.

"Hold this," she says without waiting for my answer, stubbing the filter of her cigarette between my fingers, telling me I can smoke some if I want. I do.

The girl goes face down into her bag, digging. Her fingers come out of the dark sack, tips covered in powder, soot. "Ready?" she asks, looks at me, and then she's at the side of my face. Her fingertips have the stickiness of a spider's legs. They spin out a spiral across my eyelid, stretch the webbing across my cheekbone.

"There," she says. "Done." She's smiling, proud, wants to show me, pulls a small compact from her pocket, holds it up. Except the mirror's at the wrong angle and has me out of the frame. I reach for the compact, try to pull it down but she stops my hand, holds it in hers mid-air.

She wants to know: "You like it?"

All I see is sky. "I love it," I tell her.

It might be somewhere around what used to be 3AM and the show is breaking up. There's still a small sputter of fire; a few people have stretched out around the fire pit, sleeping on their backs. Tara and I have lost the last of our time here, both blacking out after the singer went back inside and Aimee went off somewhere again. Shit Kitten said they were doing two sets but we can only remember seeing one.

You never know how long it'll take to walk across the Bloor Street bridge. Should only be a few minutes, five to eight depending how fast you are, but you never know what you might step into here. There are pockets of time, holes that'll slow you down, ghosts that'll pull you in.

Tonight the only measurement of time I have to go by is the fatigue I'm starting to feel in my lower thighs, muscles straining to get to the other side, slowed by the cold that always creeps in up here. I want to stay, lie down right where I am on the bridge, but Tara pushes into the small of my back, tells me to just move, move, move. I fall behind anyway.

Finally I crawl up the porch stairs, the last one in. Even Aimee has made it in before me, having come a different route with Trevor. No one waits to make sure I get in okay.

The legs of my jeans are damp from something wet but I don't know what. It's absorbed upwards, left a coating of black grime, tiny pebbles across the calves of my pants. I pull the jeans off and leave them in a far corner of the room, don't want anymore outside transmission on me than there already is. I throw my t-shirt there, too, wipe at my ankles. A few specks of dark sand fall onto the floor.

I find another t-shirt to wipe at my face. It's not clean but at least it's dry. The sun is starting to come up, bringing in enough light to get at my makeup. The swirl the singer painted earlier is gone, nothing left even in the crease of my eyelid.

- 13 -
EMPTY HUNGER

Aimee wakes me up and asks "Do you want to get drunk?" and I say, "Of course I do." She says, "A friend I ran into last night told me about someone who can hook us up."

I sit up. "Really? Who?"

"Well it's kind of weird," she says. "Like, how we have to pay for it."

"Okay," I say. "So what do we have to do?"

Downstairs, the kitchen sink is backed up. Blowing chunks. Looks like stewing beef, meat cut at odd angles. Tough strands of white fat exposed. A circle of blood rims the drain.

Five of us stand around trying to figure out how to deal with it, what to do. After this I think I will probably never be hungry again.

From the right, a finger runs the length of darkness beneath my skirt, distracts me from the disgust of the sink. Cam, at the back of my knees.

"What the fuck?" I spit, spinning to catch him.

He laughs. "I'm kidding," he says. "Besides, you better get used to it if you want to get drunk today."

Close your eyes and they could all be the same, guys like Cam, grabbing at ankles in the dark, hands reaching higher.

Aimee says guys always like me because I'm one of the thin girls, because they think they can just flick me away. My raccoon eyes give me away, apparently, make it too obvious that I apply insomnia in place of eyeliner.

I kick at Cam, heel to collarbone, prove Aimee wrong.

We ride west, big empty bags over our shoulders. Aimee says no one needs money anymore, that dealers just want to hold you, have someone close.

"Girls and guys?" I ask.

She shrugs. "Why not? It's not sexual. They just want to not feel so lonely or something."

A platonic exchange. No sex, just an hour in a man's arms.

"So is this different from what Trevor does?" I ask.

"Trevor does his own thing," Aimee says. "There are a lot of people who don't want to get off, just want to be cradled. Oh, and my friend said they might want to talk or something, so pretend you're listening and don't fall asleep."

Aimee pulls into a driveway in front of a line of row houses. I follow her around the back of number 133 and we knock three times, like her friend told her.

The door pulls back, opens onto a dark basement hallway. A man's moon-white face appears. The long black curls that fall around his cheeks add to the pallor. I'd guess him to be in his late thirties.

"You want something to drink?" he asks.

We smile, nod, stay silent. He steps aside and we go in.

"You girls want one bottle or two?" he asks, settling into a dirty rose-coloured couch. The legs on it have collapsed so it sits flat on the floor, bringing the man's knees up to the middle of his chest.

I look at Aimee but she's already formed an answer: "Two."

He nods. "Who's first?"

He brings me into a windowless room and tells me to get into bed. He closes the door, keeping the soft light from the hallway outside.

"I keep a knife on me at all times and guns hidden in every room," he says. "So don't think you're going to rip me off because I'll have you dead in less than a minute."

He gets in beside me and the mattress sinks to my left, rolls me against him. "Put your back to me so we can spoon," he says. I turn around and my ass crack fits against his penis. My heart drops, but bounces back again when his softness doesn't change.

He puts his head in my hair and breathes deep, sighs.

"I had a girlfriend before," he says. "I miss her."

"Oh?" I say. "What was her name?"

"Natalie," he says. "She had a body more like your friend: tall, curvy, strong."

"Uh huh," I say, and then, "sorry," not sure what I'm even apologizing for.

"It's all right," he says. "You're fine. I just like to feel someone next to me. I like skin on skin, you know?"

"Yeah," I say. "I know."

"I'm losing my energy anyway," he says. "I couldn't get it up if you paid me. I heard that's happening to other guys, too. Not that many of my friends are still around, but the ones who are . . ."

"Oh?" I say, thinking it's obviously not happening to Cam or Trevor. "What's your name?" I add.

"Mike," he says.

He's quiet for a second, doesn't ask my name. I remember Aimee's warning, about falling asleep, so I keep going. "Where'd you and Natalie meet?"

At a club, he tells me. Under the lights her mocha skin was red clay, and it cracked and flaked as she crawled across the floor. But when she looked up, smiled, she was whole again, her skin newly smooth, limbs fresh with movement. He was so high he probably didn't have access to all parts of his eyes, but could feel the warm tightness of a packed club, the guardedness stiffening in his shoulders, the small of his back. He and every other man in there had his eyes on the patch and swell of this girl's body. He remembers that he could smell the other men's crotches, the salt between the legs of the girls. Or maybe that was just the acid, heightening his senses.

He got a dance from her later, told her he loved her. Just another stoned creep at the strip club, but she went for it.

"I felt like I was the luckiest man ever that night," he says. "That night, and every night."

My jaw's tight, keeps a seal around a flood of spit behind my teeth.

Mike says his water's working today, if I want to use the bathroom. I see Aimee go into the room next as I lean into the sink, elbows propped on either side of the porcelain. Breathing deep I tell myself, *Don't puke don't puke don't puke.*

Thin tentacles of black hair zigzag out of the drain, hundreds of strands attempting to clog the flow. I run the tap and light a cigarette, wait for the water to cool down. I cup my hands and fill them, hold my breath. Pretend to drown.

The Bloor Street bridge was built above an altar, for sacrifices and worship. Below it is an eye that opens onto astral planes. The structure's belly is a skeletal system, subway tracks and frail ladders, bloated with ghost trains, rolling whispers of phantom vibrations.

My spine fits the width of the rail, the bump of each vertebrae bruising against the flat of the tracks. My shins are feathers, feet peppered with pins and needles. Beside me, Aimee dangles her legs over the edge, torso expertly balanced even with a bottle of vodka in hand. From all the way up here, you'd never believe that there's such an empty hunger running from the stretch of space between the bridge and the road below.

People used to come to this bridge to die. Jump, believing it would bring them to another world. The Eye, it only looks back at those who can see it.

When the city was built, did they think they could pave it shut? Maybe they couldn't see it. Maybe it never woke up until the bridge was built over top, hundreds of feet above. Maybe that's when the Eye knew it could finally feed.

There were so many suicides here that the city put up a payphone at one end of the bridge, a big white sign above with the number for a crisis line. "WE LISTEN 24 HOURS A DAY," the sign says, "CALL IF YOU NEED TO TALK." But would the Eye wait? Or would it close in on you anyway?

The payphone couldn't have been enough because later the barriers went up, thick silver wires creating a cage, encouraging pacing and panic attacks. But still the bridge smells of anxiety, anticlimax.

I imagine, below me now, the Eye opening through a slow, lazy spin, its size prehistoric, gaze preternatural. When the subway still ran through here I'd close my eyes as it shot out of the tunnel and into the cold shadow-light of the bridge's underside, fifteen seconds of flying over a stream of cars. The train's brakes would flare up, squeals pinging against the bridge's metal legs, its stacked weight, and every time I'd think, *This is it—today this train will go over the edge.*

Pictured from the ground up, a clumsy figure making an awkward arc in the air, its joints thick with stiffness, my own body boneless in a corner seat. An imprint, a smear of shadow, all that would be left behind.

"Let's call that number on the payphone, see what happens," Aimee says, taking another swig of vodka. We decided to crack it now, before we got back to the house. We'll tell the others we only got one bottle. No, we won't tell them anything. These will be our bottles. The others can get their own.

The bones in my back turn to chattering teeth bracing against the deep vibrations coating the belly of the bridge in goose bumps as a ghost train runs through me, as something old and dark rotates in its sleep under the crust of silent road below. I try to go boneless now but my flesh has gone tough, malnourishment cutting away at softness and curves.

My hipbone is at its highest right now. The Eye, in its state of craving, has no sense of how little there is left of me to live. Aimee stands above me, foot between my legs and hand extended. "Come on," she says.

There is a tang to the phone's mouthpiece, old words trapped in the holes of old plastic, misted spit turned sweat-sweet. The crisis line number is not toll-free: anyone without a quarter and the sense to call collect would have given up. The final confirmation that no one *really* wants to listen.

"Here," Aimee says, pulling a quarter out of a zipped pocket in her boot. There is no dial tone, but there is static, as if something is already there, eavesdropping on the other end. The quarter slides in, plunks against other coins at the bottom. Maybe we haven't been the only ones here, in this spot. Maybe they just never bothered to collect the coins near the end, either not a priority or just forgotten.

Dialing stiff buttons. Numbers three and nine crunch into their frames. Each entry still beeps through the earpiece, programmed in, maybe, rather than electrical.

Aimee's head close to mine, her ear leaning in to hear what will happen. I expect, "Please hang up and try your call again" or "We're sorry, the number you have reached is not in service." But there is only static, the chattering of more ghosts.

Below, the Eye rolls.

STRANGERS IN THE HOUSE

"My ass is going to explode," Tara says, hand over her cramping abdomen. She gulps. "I don't know if I can make it outside." She lunges off the bedroom floor, sprints. Her boots clatter down the stairs.

"One of us will have to go with her," I say.

Aimee sighs. "I'll do it."

Because you can't just go. Alone, I mean. Like cats who squat carefully and cover up, we too are vulnerable this way now. You don't want a dog to come sniffing around when you've got your pants down in the yard. You don't want your presence to linger, so you dig a hole and cover it up.

You avoid digging into any earth that's freshly turned, but it's getting hard to find untouched soil. We've been using the garden by the back door but we'll probably have to find another spot soon. That one's easy for the buddy system because one person can sit on the back steps, weapon ready, watching. As long we can keep our backs against one wall, we figure we'll be fine. There's less to guard that way.

Through the open window upstairs I can hear the pointed suck of air between Tara's teeth as she pushes through a cramp. Something wet and violent follows. Eventually she crawls back onto the mattress next to mine, sweating slightly.

"You okay?" I ask.

"I think so," she says. "I just hope I got it all out."

Aimee comes in with a stick still in her hand, now halved, its pale wood splintered at the break. "Almost got me," she says, the loose collar of her light grey t-shirt sliding off her shoulder. Her left bicep flexes below an anchor tattooed in navy blue.

this post apoc lifestyle is vague
but allows us to fill in with our
70   LIZ WORTH own nightmares

"Shit," I say.

"Told you we should just kill those dogs," Aimee says. "I have no idea why Cam will only let us hurt them if we have to."

Voices from below. Strangers in the house.

"Who's that?" Aimee asks.

"It better not be anyone wanting to stay," I say. "We've got enough people here already."

"And they could steal our stuff," Aimee says.

But downstairs it's all slow smiles, the grace of the trashed.

"These girls are cool," Cam says, as if he heard us talking upstairs. "They're living in an old club downtown." Cam's eyes are glazed, the movements of his mouth struggling through slack.

"Oh hey," one of the girls says. Her blonde hair is so greasy it looks wet and two shades darker than it should be.

"They brought presents," Cam says, turning to the girls. "Didn't you? Show them your presents."

A girl with a kitten on her shoulder holds out pinched fingers gripping soft plastic caps of grayline.

Again? I think, but then I see Aimee swallow hers.

The girl who told us her name is Brianne is showing me how to put patchouli in my pits, on the crotch of my jeans, or a light sprinkle in the pubic hair. "Keeps the scents covered, something I learned from a squeegee punk I got drunk with on Bathurst Street one summer," she says.

My fingers touch, end to end, around my forearm. Starvation. I get up and patchouli follows.

Tara has her face pressed against the window, looking to be soothed. The grayline is kicking at us hard, making us writhe. Tara's ribs show under the thin black lace of her shirt. She twists, pouts, confuses the night's slouching stars for something close to snow.

I can't remember now when the last time was we had a full day. Something that had a beginning and an end. There's no sunset we've seen recently, no moon. The stars are there, though, constellations dropping so much light there's barely any dark left to cover ourselves with. We measure time now in cigarettes and bottles and guesses, while we've still got them.

Dragged down, briefly, into a swimming blackout.

Aimee's at my elbow. "Stand up and breathe," she says, but it sounds like she's talking to Tara. Takes me a second to understand she's talking to me. In the living room Cam is drunk, sitting at the head of a circle. His words are sparks and glue. People nod, listen, rise and shout. I can't understand what he's saying but it doesn't seem like he's speaking to me anyway. He's preaching some story that's only meant to stay within his circle.

Aimee just smiles, oblivious, and flicks an eyebrow. Everyone is tripping tonight. "You feel it? You feel good?"

I do, I feel good. Except, suddenly, the back of my neck's got five pounds of hair on it and even when I hold it back phantom filaments cloak my shoulders. I can't get away from the heat.

And then a spin of the head and spots across the eyes. Outside now, puking up black string. My legs are limp behind me, sacks of fluid. Aimee's out here helping, holding me up, holding hair back while dark strands and foam hang from my chin.

Three cigarettes later a smaller darkness has come out of my head, a tangle of spiders' legs. My stomach rolls again and fresh strands fight to get past the back of my tongue. You'd never think a body could be this violent. This persistent. I don't know how I'm still puking up reams of black mass and froth on no food, nothing substantial at least. Every time another heave comes Aimee gasps for me, pants like this is trying to pull everything out of her, too.

I am a dead bulk; Aimee can barely hold me up. My eyes are mostly closed, rolling back. The night air is cold but my body holds heat throughout the trance. A narrow stream of sweat runs out of a patch of underarm hair, gets absorbed into Aimee's shoulder. She says when it hits her it's like ice, but everything I'm feeling is like fever, skin slippery, even at the knees of my jeans, spattered with foam and bile.

Aimee's got a hand on the bone between the places my breasts used to be and can feel every expansion of my lungs hitting the ribs beneath her palm. My body pitches forward again. Aimee keeps holding. Another stream trickles down from the arc of my neck. Aimee says I'm so pale I'm almost blue. Eyelids purple, blood vessels bursting from the pressure against my esophagus. My torso spasms, cheeks working up a slow spit. I ball out a final knot off the tip of my tongue. And then unconsciousness.

In my heart's left ventricle spins a dream of a small dog tied up outside a coffee shop. I bend to pet it and it jumps up, pulls against its leash. My palms cup to offer the dog something to lean into, to take the pressure off its neck. Wet winter fur between its black calloused toes lands mid-palm, as if the dog's been walking through snow, even though this dream world is as dry as the real one. This is what happens when the body craves cold: its thirst comes through in dreams, snippets of past memories cutting through the steam.

I wake, now sweating against the bedroom floor. If I could move you'd probably find a damp imprint, moisture pooled underneath my right side. I'm sure, too, that there's a black ring of filth around the outsides of my lips, like makeup gone rotten. Something's sticky and dry there but my arm's too heavy to wipe it away.

There's a white pain in my stomach, which always hurts anyway so I shouldn't really care. I try to roll onto my back but my head spins too much. I press my ear against the floor and it gets pierced by a woman's voice from somewhere else in the house. Human or spirit, I can't be sure. Either way, her moan has a violent arrow quivering through it. A scrap of my brain signals fear, but I can't run and I can't fight. I can't do anything except ease into the chill that those female cries are sending through me.

I dream within a dream, see myself talking in my sleep, saying, "What gets under the skin, what's released from your pores."

I am in my old bed, my home bed, the one before Valium, before Aimee, before now. On top of the covers, because it's too hot to be under them. I dream within a dream, see myself talking in my sleep, saying, "Unclean. Defile. Clench. Release." My astral shoulder should be at the ceiling but even my soul-body is too sick to move.

I break out of the second layer of sleep when I hear, "Wake up." I'm still on my old bed.

"Wake up," someone says again.

The window's thrown a piece of clouded sun over me. Even though the light's gone grey behind the hovering smog its stickiness is still potent. The neck of my t-shirt is ringed in sweat, and the small of my back soaks through the fabric. My eyes close and my head fills with conversations, rapid-fire and hallucinatory. Time folds over itself, elapsing.

My neck is a stiff bridge, its foundations a tired ache. I turn my head and put my ear against the floor. When my cheek rolls onto the hardwood I'm braced for a drop in temperature but it's holding just as much heat as my body's fighting off. Still, I don't turn away—not yet.

Downstairs, there's no more screaming. No sound comes through the floor now, except irregular footsteps, weak scuffles operating on vitamin deficiencies and hangovers. Five feet away, cobwebs flutter in the ribs of the old radiator, moved by a draft I can't feel. I turn flat on my back again and something crunches in my neck. Up above, a fat black spider drops from the rafters, adding to an already enormous web full of silver spun sacks, fattened dead things.

I need a cigarette but I won't even try to walk. No one expects me to have my shit together and I don't. My knees cut a path through the dust of the floor and my hands are picking up pebbles, stones pressing into my flesh.

Downstairs, Aimee helps me into a chair. When she grabs me by the pits I find strength in my legs and probably don't need her to do this. But it feels good to be touched so I let her.

She brushes hair away from my face before turning to her frying pan full of something bubbling and grim. "You hungry?" she asks.

"I don't know," I answer, lighting a cigarette from the pack sticking out of her back pocket.

"There's some bread left, peanut butter."

She must have been out to City Hall earlier, picking up another care package. At least we'll have something for another few days.

Aimee scrapes a strip of peanut butter from the side of the jar, careful not to dip too far in just yet. We don't want to run out too soon. She gets enough on the knife to spread a thin layer across a crust of bread. She tears a spot of mold off another slice and presses it all together. My stomach growls unexpectedly as she holds the food out to me. I didn't feel hungry until now. I bite in, barely tasting the peanut butter, rushing into the next bite even though the bread's dry enough to make me choke.

I get it all down. Aimee sits across from me, asks if I'm tired. I lean my head against the wall to keep the room from spinning away.

- 15 -
CHINATOWN

Cam's guests are gone but they left behind for us their coughs, curtains of phlegm shaking deep in the caves of newly infected chests.

I cannot fight, my immunity thin, flailing. New bacteria sits under the skin, threatening a scratched throat, burnout and maximized exhaustion.

Beneath the shouts of wet lungs are Tara's sobs. She's been crying in a corner for hours, riding a hard craving since Trevor told her there wasn't any grayline left.

My head hasn't moved from the spot on the wall it's rested on since Aimee last fed me. I can't hold this pose a cigarette longer.

Aimee's down to her last smoke and the latest care package didn't have any packs inside. We ride all the way to Mike's on the strength of peanut butter sandwiches.

"I want you to tell me something this time," Mike says, lips against my ear. My body reacts with a shiver and I hate myself for it.

"What do you want to know?" I ask. He sighs, like he's thinking very hard about this. I feel his chest and belly expand against me, filling the curve of my spine.

"Tell me a story," he says.

I tell him about how me and Aimee used to fall into masses of oblivion, how sometimes at the Mission we could be raised overhead by crowds of hands, cresting over droning feedback. My body always moved like it had been through this before, had the familiarity of being saved. Aimee's stayed stiffer, on guard, braced for the floor as she sailed towards the stage, the soles of her Docs blurring over skulls, delicate faces. And around me, in the audience, bodies shook in time to a one-two beat, faces held high in salute to a boy whose face was red, a boy who screamed and screamed for us.

One night we were outside, between sets. The buzz of the last band had gotten in our ears, followed us everywhere. We didn't know this was called tinnitus. We thought we were just meant for it, made for it. That the music sunk into us, that we kept it alive.

It was December, two nights before Christmas. Half a foot of snow had fallen since we'd gotten to the Mission but it was too hot inside with all the energy buzzing around. Half the club had crowded onto the sidewalk, staining ice crystals with their boots and cigarette butts. Half the filth of the city stamped on a single corner.

Against the wall, a girl holding her hair, holding half of herself up. In my head it felt like it should already be two in the morning. A circle had formed in front of the stage. A group of guys were using the bare floor to slip onto their tailbones and slide on the studs of their thick silver belts. Their girlfriends laughed each time they went down, and the circle got wider each time someone's drink got spilled.

Above us, the last band sounded tired. Old. We were bored. It was the last show of the year. Aimee was staying at her cousin's house then. Her cousin and her husband were older, and they'd invited her to stay for a couple weeks over Christmas. She asked if I wanted to come back with her that night, sleepover. There was a liquor cabinet, she promised, and Christmas wine, gifted and opened for early guests, leftover on the kitchen counter and in the side door of the fridge.

We snuck beers out of the club to drink on the ride out to the city's furthest edge. Aimee's cousin lived an hour away by public transit, a single streetcar ride but a long one in bad weather. The snow that night, it kept falling. A foot on the ground by last call.

The house was a fifteen-minute walk from the nearest streetcar stop. When we got off, the snow was untouched. At the city limits, it was easy to take one step outside at night and believe, entirely, that you were the only person left in the world.

Winter wetness got into the tops of our boots, chilled the steel toe caps. The front of our jeans were packed white. I slipped, came down hard on a patch of black ice. My beer bottle, still half-full, shattered in my parka pocket, and the smell of it instantly dripped through. Aimee, drunk, dipped her hand into my coat and scooped out a fistful of glass, kept walking. The next day my ass would be bruised, an entire cheek tinted blue, but Aimee's hand was perfectly intact, not a scratch of crimson marring the palm.

At the house we helped ourselves to half a bottle of red, half a bottle of white, and a box of chocolates, all already opened. Aimee only ate two candies but I couldn't stop, not even when I felt them solidify at the back of my throat, a globule of sugar I could scarcely push through.

We had to smoke outside. We were wasted by the time of our last smoke of the night, a necessary ritual to keep the nicotine levels going to sleep through eight hours.

I shivered in my parka, its lower half still wet from the busted beer. Aimee wobbled, could barely stand. I asked if I could brush my teeth. To get the sugar off, at least. Aimee said to use her toothbrush, pointed the way to the bathroom on her way up the stairs.

The lights were off in the bedroom when I got there, Aimee already passed out. The smell of beer clung all around us.

In the morning the middle of my calf was streaked with a light russet trail of dried Labatt 50. I swung myself out of bed. Beside me, Aimee stayed still. She was always at her heaviest in her sleep.

My legs were bare but my parka was still wrapped around my shoulders, bunched at the wrists. Beneath the covers, a wealth of brown glass glinted.

Mike gives us each a pack of smokes and a mickey of gin. Aimee asks if he knows where we can get any grayline but all he says is, "Maybe, but I'd stay away from that stuff."

"Too late," we tell him, assuming his maybe means yes.

We ride back through Chinatown and see a restaurant with people in it.

"Wow," Aimee says, slowing down across the street. "It looks like it's open, like they're serving."

We're both hungry again.

"Let's go," Aimee says.

Cam and Trevor heard rumours of a few restaurants that never closed, surviving on old grease, dried fat and rain water for boiling the meat of feral cats and stray dogs, just like those urban legends of Chinese restaurants that were serving lost pets in their chow mein.

We are more restless than wary. Hunger is secondary, but it's pushing through as soon as the smell of food hits us. Stomachs growl. The warmth of a steaming counter cuts through the dampness of the day. There are five other people seated at tables, two men in the window and three in a corner. They eye us but keep their chins to their plates.

The menu is sparse. Most of it has been blacked out by marker, leaving noodles, rice, and meat. We order the noodles and pay in cigarettes, five each.

Aimee leans back in her chair and slides her boots off, puts her feet in my lap. Her socks have turned grey and her toes flash pink through the holes in their tops.

No one in the restaurant talks. There is no music playing in the background, no buses chugging by outside. Without the voices of others filling in the blanks for us, we cautiously stretch into the void as two steaming bowls slide in front of us. The noodles glisten between chopsticks, slide out of the slick grip, and eventually I give up and grab for a chunk of the lavender-grey meat that's been laid overtop.

"I didn't know this came with meat," Aimee says. She turns to the counter. "Excuse me? Excuse me?" The cook looks up but doesn't smile. "Excuse me? What kind of meat is this?" The cook looks down, shakes his head, worries a cloth over an imaginary spot on the counter.

The meat squishes between my teeth. Bland juice squirts across my tongue.

Aimee is rolling a piece of meat around in her mouth, face hesitant. Whatever it is, she doesn't want to let it inside of her and instead spits it down the side of the table, onto the floor. If anyone notices, they don't say anything.

A rush of saliva helps me get mine down, even though I immediately regret swallowing it and wish I had done like Aimee.

"I wonder if this *is* where the wild dogs end up when they die," she asks, tackling a strand of white in her bowl.

Aimee and I clamp our noodles and slurp at the same time. They are salt and rubber, tunneling bodies squirming on tongues. Our bowls are full of worms, wriggling. Over my shoulder, the two men in the corner lift their last mouthfuls, long white noodles hanging limp.

"I can't eat this," I say.

Aimee's already pushed hers away. She waits at the counter while I walk to the washroom, hoping for water, just something to splash my face with. The stench keeps me from getting both feet inside. The toilet is full to the top, floating with brown and yellow. Gobs of toilet paper have soaked into a deep gold along the top. In front of it, a tall red bucket, it too full of human water and waste. Around the back and base of the toilet are low piles of old bunches of toilet paper and napkins and torn newspaper pages, all smeared with dried shit.

I could gag but trace amounts of remaining grayline won't let me. It keeps the throat and esophagus as tight and tense as the rest of the body, everything on high alert.

Aimee is already outside, waiting by our bikes. We zigzag between lines of dead cars along Spadina Avenue, coasting tight between their warts of rust. They'll slice you good, those cars.

We stop on the porch of a torched house and break into the gin. The smokes are fresh, for once, and the first drags hit us as if they're the first ones we've had all day. Aimee tests her weight on the wooden boards before lying all the way back. We keep the bottle tucked between us, in case anyone passes by and asks for a sip. Not that we've seen anyone since the restaurant, but you never know. We're three shots in, each, when we hear, "Hey!"

We sit up too fast. Heads rush, underlining an early buzz. We look ahead but see no one.

"Hey!" It comes again. "Up here."

An arm waves from a window next door, a dirty blonde head calling us over. "Me and my sister are *dy*ing to talk to someone else," she says. "We've been stuck with each other for *days*."

The two girls lie together on the same bed. Close up the dirty blonde looks like she might be younger than I thought. Her hair's streaked with grease and she's left her blue denim shirt unbuttoned. A plain white bra underneath is striped with dark yellow sweat.

"I'm Carla. This is Jenna," she says, pointing to the darker haired girl. They don't look like sisters at all. Jenna's hair is thick, wavy, her skin a deeper tone than Carla's.

Carla pulls something out of her shirt pocket that looks like a joint. She lights it up with a wooden match but when it starts to blaze it doesn't smell like pot. More like incense—cinnamon and jasmine. She offers me a pull. Its taste is mild and white, like chalk.

"What is this?" I ask.

Carla shrugs. "Our roommate got it for us. I can't remember what it's called." She looks at Jenna for help, but Jenna just stares ahead, doesn't even make an effort to answer. "I think he said it was called 'ashelle.' Whatever it is, it's good. Better than weed."

"Yeah," Jenna says, finally.

Carla laughs at her sister. "The ashelle's on her, that's why she's so quiet."

It must be on me, too, because everything Carla says makes her sound like she talking through an underwater helmet.

Sweat's collected along Aimee's upper lip. I thirst for it, lean into her. She lets me stay on her face.

When I pull away, Carla's face has split sideways she's grinning so wide. "The ashelle's on you, too," she says, and rubs Aimee's back. "Just go with it," she says, over and over.

Rare for Aimee to have a bad trip, I'd told Carla when it hit. I think of the mickey in my bag, wondering if the alcohol had anything to do with it.

"It's a good buzz, right?" Carla asks Aimee. I know what she's doing: mind control, hypnosis of the trip. It's an old trick but one we've all had to use before.

Since my kiss with Aimee my mouth has been secreting salt, limbs threatening seizure. I want another shot but don't want to share. Just because Carla gave something to us doesn't mean we have to do the same.

"It's a good buzz," Aimee says.

I manage to count the spark of matches around me. Eight cigarettes later, at six minutes a cigarette, must be bringing us to close to an hour into this buzz. The salt in my mouth has mostly been swallowed. My vision is something less than blind. I sit up.

"Now you'll really start to feel good," I hear Carla say to Aimee.

Finally, Aimee asks, "Do you want to get out of here?" and I realize I'd been waiting for those words, because, yes, I do.

Back at the house there's a girl grinding Cam's crotch. Me and Aimee are still buzzing, but we can't tell if it's from whatever it was we smoked earlier, or if it's from the rest of the mickey we killed on the way back.

Every voice in the house is amplified. "Want to go to the third floor?" Aimee asks.

No one's been to the third floor since Brandy and Camille were up there. The windows are stained glass, smaller than the windows in the rest of the house. The light seems only to hit the blue panes, holding everything in frosted incandescence. I have to duck my head under the low ceiling, wonder if the walls are shrinking in on us.

Aimee wobbles to the center of the room and flops to the floor. Her eyes roll around in their sockets too slowly, like someone's poured syrup all over them. She lights a cigarette and exhales a dragon cloud of smoke. With her head tilted back I can see gaps where she's missing teeth. Must be recent, those losses. Mine aren't loose yet, but they will be soon enough.

"So this is it," Aimee says. I can tell she's fighting to focus her eyes on the corners of the room to watch for moving shadows.

Tara comes up the stairs. "You two were gone forever," she says.

"Really? How long?" I ask. The words are slower in my mouth than they should be.

Tara doesn't answer. Instead, "Look what I got off Cam." She holds out a joint. I can smell the weed. It's the real thing.

"Really? He gave that to you?"

"Well, no, not really. I took it from him," she says. "So don't tell, k?"

She lights up and inhales, bends close to offer her mouth and breathe it all into my lungs. Her legs are bare, glowing blue in the light of the room as she shifts towards Aimee to pass her the joint. Aimee barely registers. Tara shrugs and sits back beside me.

"You fucked up or what?" she says.

But before I make a move to answer, a wing sprouts from Tara's leg. It starts with dark brown stems and then pops out turquoise tips, white feathers freckled with grey and black. Tara doesn't move, too busy holding smoke in her chest. The wing is long enough for it to beat against the floor. It flaps until it falls off of Tara's leg, becomes bodiless, independent.

This is when I decide to go back downstairs.

The pot smoke's brought the noise level down from where it was when I first got here. Cam's still with the girl, says her name is Melanie. He found her hanging around outside and invited her in. He likes to believe he's saving people sometimes. I can tell by looking at her she's the kind of girl who's always bumming cigarettes without bothering to remember your name. Wonder she's made it alive this long.

Cam says, "Melanie's gonna stay with us tonight."

Brandy's been too sick to speak lately but now she steps up, her studded jacket clanking. "Just tonight though right, Cam?" she says from the door.

We all maintain unspoken rules. Visitors are fine, but they can't live here. We've only got so much. One extra person means less moldy bread to go around.

"I told you to get off my case," Cam says.

Brandy pulls half her face behind the doorframe and glares, but it's Melanie's face that's red, gone timid.

"I have a place you know," Melanie says, the statement only vaguely directed at the room. "I was just gonna crash because, you know, Cam asked me, that's all."

Aimee interrupts any further conversation by walking in. Her eyes are so glazed they could leak. Her hand is out, extended for Melanie's. The girl's hand stays limp but her eyes are wired to the pointed bone of Aimee's wrist, the fox skull tattooed over her veins. Neither of them offer their names. No one else offers introductions.

Aimee pulls me onto her lap and wraps her legs around my back. My throat is still tender from the drugs upstairs but I can't stop another wave of high from hitting me and then every inch of potential noise that's left in the city is collecting in a single building—our house—and we're building it all, breathing it all in through thick droplets of air, me and Aimee in one corner admiring the oiled silk of our dirty hair, the way hers glints gold and red and mine casts snow even in the thud of light, and in another corner, Cam's got a semicircle going around the back of the room and the only word they keep saying is survival survival survival survival survival until it's a prayer, a practice in hypnosis. And Brandy and Carrie are still wearing their studded jackets, playing the same song over and over, a chant in counterbalance to Cam's, the Exploited hurling sex and violence and sex and violence and sex and violence from a tinny boombox and I can't believe someone's salvaged batteries just for that because I always hated that song but love it right now because the sounds we thought would be with us always, in either world, old or new or dying, couldn't follow us here because so many of us forgot to save things like batteries or ran them down too early. And everything gets louder and louder between the walls that we've declared to be ours until we own what we believe, in this moment, to be the last wall of sound that will ever exist and we are responsible for it and we are responsible for it and we are responsible for it.

We lose time, like usual, and speculate about UFOs: alien abduction, identity theft, physical probing into supernatural phenomenon of the six-six-sixth senses.

Melanie hasn't slept since she got here. You can smell it on her, the night sweat that clings to sleeplessness and burnout. If she's overstayed her one-night welcome none of us know for sure.

Melanie's soles have armour. They're so calloused they scrape the floor, wake us up in what we guess might be the morning.

I remember her saying, at some point in the night, that she likes the boots we all wear, us girls.

"Can I try a pair?" she asked. Tara had a newer pair, recently looted, still stiff.

"Here, you can break these in for me," she said to Melanie, handing them over by their laces like stiff kittens dangling by their scruffs.

"Cool," Melanie said, sliding her naked foot inside the hard leather.

Today she's gliding over the floor, keeping her legs straight. Tara's boots have eaten into Melanie's heels. She stops every few feet just to take a drag of her cigarette, which I saw her sneak from Cam's pack. She accentuates her inhalations with the pain of her blisters.

My head is broken up into aching compartments and my mouth is coated with whiskey piss. I want Melanie to quiet the fuck down.

"What. Are. You. Doing," I ask her.

"My feet are fucked up," she says. "It hurts to walk."

"Why don't you try crawling?"

Not that I could walk either right now. I can only smoke, already too awake from these few words. I puff out a perfect circle. A fat O floats over my face.

Melanie lays her cheek on the edge of my mattress. She asks for a drag even though she just put a cigarette out. She's on all fours now. I was only joking when I suggested she crawl.

The swelling of her Achilles tendon has plumped up and bruised the soft grooves of her ankle, filling out the curves between round and thin bones. A blister has broken, leaking something clear and sticky. Its center is black and its outline screams with temper.

"I think it's infected," she says, following my eyes. A curl of smoke gets in my gaze and the world goes lopsided. We don't have supplies to spare to clean her up.

"You shouldn't wear boots with no socks on," Tara says, walking up behind Melanie. "The steel will wear right through the inner lining and scrape against your toes, take your nails right off. I've seen it happen."

Melanie just pushes out her jaw and stares.

"We could leave, you know."

I say this to Aimee as I finger the key to my parents' house, still in my pocket. We are in Aimee's bed, spooning.

"Do you think we could do it? Be on our own, I mean?" she asks.

"Why not?"

"It's less protection, less connections."

"But maybe things could be better somewhere else." As I say this, a thud vibrates through the house, like something—or some-one—heavy just fell hard against a wall.

"I heard they still have chocolate in Montreal," Aimee says. "And I heard part of their subway still runs sometimes."

Downstairs someone's either laughing or crying. Or both.

"I wasn't thinking that far, but—"

"So where?"

"My parents' house. It's empty. It could be ours. We don't have to stay there all the time, but just for a little bit. Just to get away from this."

"But what about food? Picking up care packages?"

"What about privacy? What about doors we can lock?"

"Okay," Aimee says. "We can go."

- 16 -
FROM THE INSIDE OUT

No goodbyes, no information. We don't want anyone to know where we are. We don't want anyone to follow us.

Tara's made it easy to avoid her. She woke up with her hand out, asking to go and do a pick up with us. Me and Aimee agreed we'd never go to a dealer's place alone. We should do the same for Tara but we don't, instead told her we had to meet someone today, "a friend we promised to help." So she left a little while ago. We don't ask if she went with anyone.

No one's seen what we've put into the bags on our backs. No one knows we've taken all we can. And so no one asks when we pick our way to our bikes. No one asks if, or even when, we'll be back.

It's raining when we get outside. We cup our hands and drink from a bucket of rainwater in the yard before we push off. The hydration goes right to my head, clarifies.

We ride.

We're breathless by Queen and Portland. Aimee's at her calf, wiping at a cut that opened from the graze of a rusting car.

"Should I be worried?" she asks. "Like, is tetanus an actual thing?"

I shrug. "I don't know. Didn't we all have to get shots for that?"

"Yeah," Aimee says. "Maybe."

"You shouldn't be out here."

The voice comes from behind me, belongs to a head of red hair shot with grey, a chin that's pocked with early signs of aging.

There used to be a club here, its entrance adorned in spires, wrought iron spirals. The door's off its hinges now, metal links bent at impossible angles. In its place a curtain, four inches of it drifting off the doorframe, enough to show the dancefloor. I see one, two, three pale bodies on their backs. One of them moans, rolls over.

"Come inside."

The request comes from inside the club, but it's too dark to see who it's coming from.

"Nice boots, wanna fuck?"

Through the slit of the curtain I can see a bloated body crawling limbless like a slug, one eye shut and the other sitting low on a distended cheek, mouth an exaggerated sag.

"Go," someone says.

We get back on our bikes and we ride, take short breaks every few miles. Even when we were at our most nourished, this ride would have been hard for our smokers' lungs, boozers' endurance. Between breaths come the excited gasps over clean sheets, quiet rooms and privacy.

We turn left onto my old block and stop at the neighbour's yard. The front window's been smashed out, frame clean of any panes, but there are still patches of pale green in the grass. Aimee scoops out a fistful by the roots and hands me a chunk. "Eat it," she says, "so we don't get scurvy."

The corpse of a cat is only a few feet away from where the blades of grass grew. Its belly is a dried slit, but the blood's yet to trade all of its red for brown. "Looks fresh," Aimee says, chewing through her words.

Russet circles of toothless stains have spread across the bed-spread in my parents' bedroom. Were they there a few days ago? Am I so contaminated that I left behind an imprint?

Aimee's oblivious, lying back, right hand in the dead center of a stain. The comforter looks like it carries a contagion factor, like it's leaking from the inside out. There are stains on the floor and ceiling, too, but they're smaller, easier to avoid, which is what I do as I will the house to settle around me.

Something scrapes against a wall a floor below—a fingernail or a picture frame. Something with just enough of an edge to catch on our nerves.

Both of us at the same time: "Did you hear that?"

Darkness falls. Like the house has placed a phantom hand over our eyes. A finger catches in the dip of my throat, presses. I try to push it away but nothing's there.

The foundation gives, tilts the house to the left.

"Ang?" Aimee says.

It's still daylight but everything's gone black, as if the darkness is coming from the house itself.

Something like a man's breath is at my cheek. It comes at the moment when I know I truly have nothing anymore, not even the hope of spending one night in this house. Ever since the flames became the same colour as the sky, this city has been stealing my sleep, cutting at the youth that used to be my face. Black and curls of orange could have filled us in seconds but instead, we ran. If I'd known we were running just to be left with nothing, maybe I wouldn't have moved so quickly.

Something oozes out of the carpet beneath my knees. Something else drips onto Aimee's hair. The house is rotting at hyper-speed.

The ceiling fan comes down on Aimee. "Shit!" she says.

"Are you okay?" I ask.

"I don't know."

Pressure on my chest. The phantom's angry finger, its silent accusations, poking a throbbing trail down the front of me. What do you do when there are no more rules? What do you when nothing is what it used to be?

You give in, you give up, you get out, or you get up.

I used to know the staircase by heart, walked it a hundred times drunk in the pitch dark. I've let too much time pass to keep it all in my head. I miss the very first step and tumble down. Aimee is only seconds behind.

We crawl to the front door because the house won't let any light in even from the windows downstairs. Outside, the blindfold lifts, vision is restored. We fly off the front steps just as the tip of the roof caves in, the rest of the house collapsing beneath it.

When there are no more rules, it's hard to tell whether you should cry or just move on. For now, we just move.

SELECTIVE MEMORY

Trevor's let a dog into the house. It tore through a gap in the door, salivating at his heels.

Lucky for us, Cam just happened to be in the kitchen and came down on the dog hard with a cast iron frying pan. We knew we'd find a use for that thing one of these days.

The dog fell, unconscious, its head a block of brown fur and ear mites. Satisfied it would be still for at least a few minutes, Cam turned and brought his fist to Trevor's face.

Lucky for Trevor, Aimee rushed forward just a little faster than I did, seconds which made all the difference in yanking at Cam's t-shirt sleeve just in time to steer the punch clear of Trevor's nose.

"What the FUCK were you thinking?" Cam yells, red-faced, words flying with the same ferocity as the dog's.

"I—I'm sorry," Trevor says through a quiver in his chin. His hand shakes as he pushes a stringy chunk of hair behind his ear.

"Fuck!" Cam says, spitting the exclamation onto the floor. The glob lands beside the dog's paw, splatters an outer claw. "Just get the fuck out of my face for a little bit, okay?"

Trevor nods, but keeps his head down, eyes from Cam. "Okay."

"Why do you hang out with Cam so much, anyway?" Aimee asks Trevor upstairs as she pulls on another joint Tara had tucked away in her bra.

"Probably for the same reasons you stay here," Trevor says.

Cam envisions himself a child-man soldier growing an army of deviants who will cultivate and dominate what remains at the end of the world. It's delusion. Or illusion. Ill, at any rate, and what we're all living with to some extent.

"He knows where to find things. He has connections I could never have made on my own. He showed me how to hold a knife so the blade doesn't break. He showed me how to stab a stick through a body on the first try. And he's not all bad, really, once you get to know him a little more. He can be nice. He's just had a lot of rough times. It's not his fault he's fucked up."

"Oh my God," Tara says through a veil of smoke. "You *like* him."

Trevor smiles, looks away. "No," he says. "I mean, you know how Cam is about—"

"Oh we know," Aimee says.

"—and besides, it would never—"

"But just because it would never happen, or never work, doesn't mean you still can't feel," I say. "You wouldn't be the first person to want what they can't have."

"I don't, though," Trevor says. "I don't."

"Okay," we all say, nodding in agreement.

Trevor tokes, leans forward into our circle. "Don't tell anyone we talked about this, k?"

Cam calms down, and Trevor disappears back downstairs. Tara crashes out at the back of a walk-in closet. She headed that way about an hour ago, her eyes swimming for focus, mouth a maraschino cherry brightly chewed. The rest of her, legless, muscles tenderized as if someone's kneaded powdered lithium right into the meat of her. It's probably just heat stroke, but you never know.

None of us are drinking today. Alcohol to a dry mouth chokes like cracked black pepper swallowed too fast.

The buzz from that joint has disappeared and I don't know where the next one will come from. Sobriety is exhausting. Doesn't give any of the numbness of alcohol and keeps everything on the surface.

Today it's dredging up hazel eyes and narrow hips. Hunter's hands and the questions they hold for me:

Have you ever had days when you didn't think you could survive any other way than to become something built out of torn skin and teeth, all elbows and drudgery?

If you fail to die when you are supposed to, does it destroy the order of the earth?

Aimee used to ask me if I ever think of Hunter. I'd lie and tell her no, and eventually she'd quit the question. But I couldn't tell her yes, because it would only make memories stronger, harder to black out if I kept reinforcing them with words.

In case I die in another day or two, I try to feel out for his spirit, to see if he's close, waiting to help take me over. I used to imagine him standing right behind me, or watching me from a spot on the ceiling. I haven't thought of that in a long time. I reach out, but feel nothing.

There's so much I've tried to blank out. Experimented with selective memory, envied amnesia patients and afternoon television plots. If I could forget the disappointment in my mom's voice and the concern in her eyes. Or the guilt of once having a childhood. And the recurring reminders of what can't be undone. The first morning I woke up beside Hunter and curled between his arms. The loss of identity when I questioned whether I'd ever really wanted to die. The confusion when Aimee's friendship made me want to live. The hopelessness in finding an easy answer.

I did forget things, but none of what I'd made an effort to erase. I forgot people's faces, names. Forgot I'd ever met them, made out with them. It was easy to laugh off, just giggle and feign popularity. Assume that kind of bullshit behaviour was acceptable because I'd been dating one of the best-known singers on the scene. I knew everybody, but couldn't possibly be expected to remember anybody.

I even forgot them when I spent six months trying to cover up the remnants of Hunter's kisses with the spit of strangers. Anoint and cleanse.

You know what? I remember them all now. Every face. Every prick of stubble of their chins. I remember where we stood when we pushed our tongues together and the rush of wet when a hand went down my pants.

As everything else disappears, the memories come rushing back. Every boy that ever crossed my hips and every word that left my lips and every look I gave and every one I got back.

These were all the things I thought I'd lose forever. I've let them all back in. There are just so many people who aren't around anymore. What I remember of them is all that's left.

The room stifles. My hair is sticking to my skin. Brushing it away, I can smell my underarm.

I fall asleep and dream within a dream. A spiral in the sand. One spiral leads to another to another to another, and from those come worms, each thicker than the last, all glistening. Sand flakes off their bodies. Their mouths are wide, trying to scream.

It's the exposure. They never wanted to break through the surface. The next worm I uncover will have a voice and I don't want to hear what it sounds like.

I've been sitting on my heels, feet and legs tucked under me, drawing the spirals that drew the worms out. My legs are jelly, no blood in them anymore. It takes a strobe light of strength to get them out from under me.

I finally swing my legs out, sit with them crossed instead, making sure the sides of my shoes brush away the spirals in the process, closing doors I shouldn't have opened.

I wake, still dreaming of a cold moon, low in the sky, its pale pink shadow twin peering out from behind it.

My face is in the sand. The moon's cratered face is a grimace, features fallen. It has its eyes on me. The skin along my right arm rises with bumps, hairs on end. An electric chill.

Down at the beach there are voices followed by a hard-edged laugh, a sound with too many blades to belong to either of them. I stand and start running. Not because anything I see or hear tells me to run, but because something inside me just knows to do it.

I wake, for real this time, snagged off the night beach on shards of words spurting up from the floor below. For a second I think it's the ghost in the basement. It takes a full sentence before I recognize the voice as Cam's. Aimee answers him, but

I can't hear what she's saying. She keeps her voice lower than his.

Footsteps on the stairs, moving fast, and then Cam's face is in mine. He's gotten mean again. His face his red, lined with anger. I don't want him this close to me but I don't have the strength to move. I wonder how he does it, maintaining his strength. Maybe it's just adrenaline.

I brace myself for the boom of his voice but instead he gurgles, scrapes phlegm from deep in his chest. Spits a green gob on the wall above my head. I close my eyes and hear it connect, feel the spray. I open my eyes and he's already gone.

Aimee comes in with a glass of cloudy water for us to share. It smells like earth. I swallow my half in two gulps.

She frowns at Cam's spit on the wall, which has slid down a couple of inches from where it landed and started to dry to the paint.

"I don't know what his problem is," she says before I have the chance to ask. She hands me her bandana to wipe it up. "I'd help you get it off but I feel sick just looking at it."

I double up the cloth so I don't have to feel the firmer lumps of mucus. I dig a hole in the front yard and bury it so the dogs aren't attracted to the smell.

The air outside feels good. Better than inside. There are dark clouds moving in, shadows of rain. The closest thing to optimism we might have for a while.

Cam is at the front window, watching me. I decide not to go back into the house, at least for now.

I close my eyes and ask, "Where should I go?" My dream comes back to me and the answer that comes is: "Go where there used to be water. Go where the lake once stood."

The beach is dry, just miles of rock and sand now. Even if the lake were still here, it would be too polluted to drink from, or even bathe in.

Still, I wish for the hypnosis of the tide, a sound that could distract me from everything I don't want to think about, and from everything I'd rather not be living through.

I imagine water on rock, wiping my thoughts away. Instead I get a vision of white on white, ripped satin and crinoline, a stained slip imitating marrow.

The vision manifests as Shelley and Anadin, two girls who live down here in an old beach house.

Anadin: People get us confused. Believe us to be twins. Me, in long black hair, off-white lace. Shelley, white-blonde and always in antique slips, feet bare and beautiful.

Shelley: Anadin's the one whose head snaps when she feels eyes.

Ang: They send me a vision of sand, dead water. Birds that can't breathe, suffocated, mid-flight, their hollow bones too weak against the weight of smog.

Shelley: No one comes down here, to the beach. They're too afraid of what the water's left behind. It all looks so empty. It'll make you believe you're alone, but things follow you here. And they'll follow you out.

Anadin: We haven't seen another girl in so long. And now this one who's here, well, we knew right away we wanted her.

Shelley: Ang shouldn't have had eyes. She would have been stronger without them.

Ang: I found braids of psychic debris. Shelley, a girl in furs, all head and bone, teetering on spokes of ankles. Anadin, her sister, held together by a long string of pearls, bound in delicate underwear. Their arms, whips. Their faces younger than they should have been.

Anadin: Ang, a wisp. Barely able to stand up under the weight of her own dreams. Our arms wrapped around her.

Ang: They had been picking up shells and glass smoothed by waves. Oracles, they said. They asked if they could show me what they meant. I said yes.

Shelley: The End was caused by an omen misaligned. A coagulation of a frequency pitch that's needled into everyone's ears, settled permanently.

Anadin: It was a miscalculated rule of thirds. Cyber energy and radio transmissions dead and released, bound.

Ang: They invited me in. Their place an ancient beach house filled with antique birdcages. Feathers and bones. They pulled out husks of still wings from behind golden doors, held them to my face so I could see how the connective tissue was starting to show through. A contrast of sharp white and black shine, they said. Something they said would make beautiful jewelry after the process of decay was complete.

Anadin asked me if I wanted to hold it, put it back to rest in the cage. I cut myself on a stiff beak reaching into the confines of thin bars. Blood that looked as thin as I felt beaded between the hairs of my arm.

Shelley: Ang told us about where she lives, about the care packages. We gave up on food years ago. Losing that habit has kept us out of touch. We'd forgotten that people wouldn't understand what had happened.

Ang: Shelley unwrapped her ballet slipper, pointed her foot to me. The skin of her baby toe, covered in fish scales, skin sharpened to a grey glint.

Shelley: The diatribe, it came out as rust at first. Not a conspiracy theory, but a leveling. A cleansing.

Anadin: A belief in the strongest. Of who will be left. Of who's made it this far without meaning to. Structural pyramids ignored.

Shelley: Something that barely needs to be spoken. As in: If you don't know, we're not telling.

(Here, an aside, as Anadin and Shelley confess: We are always half-blind and fully drunk on these words. We've tried to write them down, but as they come out we start to wobble. Haven't managed more than a scribble. That's why we prefer oral.)

Anadin: Cataclysm. Simultaneous and personal.

Ang: Translation: *It will chew you up and shit you out.*

Shelley: But you are not alone.

Anadin: We are not alone.

Shelley: Choices are facing extinction. Soon there will only be basic instinct and muscle memory to carry you when The End nears the final phase of its cycle. And it will come. Possible psychological effects might include guilt, anxiety, depression, suicidal tendencies. Guaranteed psychological effects include alcohol and drug abuse. Possible physical effects include life, or death.

Ang: It's my body and I'll die if I want to.

- 18 -
POST-SACRED

My head is a bubble of hypoglycemia, but at the beach that doesn't matter. It doesn't matter that I don't have parents anymore, either, because here I can at least have sisters.

I am curled in Anadin's lap, her hand in my hair, twisting strands around her finger. My hair has never been this long before. Never long enough to play with. I've spent what felt like a night here and now it's warm outside but Anadin and Shelley are both still in furs. I can smell the skins, primordial in their early rot.

Shelley is silent. "Observing," Anadin says.

"Observing what?" I ask.

"We are post-sacred now," Anadin says. And then: "What a time to be living in."

My chest vibrates with a bronchial cough. Anadin smoothes my forehead. I pretend the air is full of sea salt, that breathing alone is enough to cleanse me, cure me.

There is a vile trail where the tide shriveled up, as if the shoreline was shaken with the dense hack of its own infected lungs. The sky's peeling back a shade, an animal lightening its coat of water. I ask Anadin, "Do you sleep?" I don't know why I ask this. It's not until after it's out of me that I realize it's even on my mind.

"Sometimes," she says. "We get tired from dancing to our own images in a mirror."

A mild chill runs through my left arm but the rest of my body still sweats. Anadin twirls another chunk of hair and I drift somewhere close to half-sleep, something deep enough to dream. In my dream Shelley and Anadin are gone. I'm looking down the beach to see if I can spot them. The sand's smooth, no sign of footprints, as if a phantom tide has come and cleared everything away. I want to make a wish. I twirl a grain of sand between my thumb and finger and focus on what I want. I worry that because I can't ask for just one thing my wish won't come true.

I wake up. My head's in Shelley's lap now. Anadin's kneeling by my ankles. Her hands are at my waist, pulling my skirt up, my panties off.

She smiles at me and I smile back as the cotton slides down my thighs, over my knees. I kick my underwear away when they get around my feet.

Anadin's fingers disappear into the cavern between my thighs. There's nothing left in there. The End sucked it all up. Anadin's fist disappears inside me and I don't even feel it, but I want to.

She pulls out and opens up her hand. In her palm, a silver charm in the shape of a heart. "For luck," she says. "Remember?"

I fall asleep again and a storm rolls in. Drenches the beach, the streets. Shelley and Anadin are gone. So are my panties. It's a warm rain. I stay where I am and let the water run over me.

I get back to the house after the rains. I walk straight to the back, grab a bike, and go before anyone sees me. I break my promise with Aimee and go see Mike. As I ride away, a dog's bark is muffled inside the walls of the old Victorian.

When I lie down my skirt hikes up. The room's probably too dark for Mike to see, but I wonder what he can feel through his cargo shorts.

The scent of his hair is stronger today, foul with oil. I hold each breath for as long as possible as he climbs against me.

His arm comes across my chest. His nose rests against the back of my neck. He sighs, and then says, "Tell me a story."

I wasn't expecting this again. I just thought he'd talk for a while, or that we'd just lie here.

"Really?" I say.

"Yeah," he says. "You're picking up for your friends, too, right? There's extra for that."

"What do you want me to tell you about?" I ask.

"Anything," he says. "It'll help me not to think too much for a while."

I tell him it was a peep-toe peepshow back at this place I lived in for a summer, above a dive bar with no name, just a big Labatt Blue sign in their window.

I had no air conditioning and the city was exhausted with the summer. Exhumed. It was so hot everything stuck to us, whole days swirled down the shower drain daily.

Me and Aimee dealt with it in short-shorts and hot pink underwear, t-shirts that snuggled lightly around our breasts but never traveled much further. She'd come over and we'd get drunk, hang our legs out the window and let the men in the bar downstairs howl up at our feet spiked in metallic stilettos: gold for me, silver for Aimee. The ridges of the window tract dug into the backs of our knees, but we made sure to stay drunk enough not to feel it.

"Was your life always fun like that?" Mike asks.

"Sometimes," I say. "Sometimes."

I tell him about how it might have been different if I hadn't left a corpse of ego out by the ocean. I tell him I was happiest when I had forgotten there was a world before 2PM. I tell him about small, crowded stages. I tell him about songs shrouded in reverberation. I tell him about bands I used to know and love that didn't play music: they played our lives, connected knees to shins at all angles. I tell him about words that nudged and smudged the shine of our eyelids in a silver preamble, lyrics built out of the gradient of recovered memories and the breakdown of exposure. I tell him that we wore it all like a shield. Still do, though mostly only in our heads now, reduced to what we can remember. I tell him too much, but in the end he gives me everything I want: vodka, cigarettes and half a sheet of acid.

"It sounds like you've been through enough to know where this stuff can take you," he says.

I ride back slowly, stopping to drink. I'll share everything with Aimee and some with Trevor and Tara, but I need a little for myself after everything I put into this.

Aimee's in the kitchen, where there's a miracle of a blue gas flame in the stove.

"Cam found some food," she says, pointing to powdered eggs and dried milk, a bag of flour full of dead moths. "We'll just pick them out," she adds.

My mouth thickens with appetite. The pan sizzles. Aimee stirs but the fork's prongs come away tinged with pink.

"What the fuck?" she says.

The powdered eggs are turning red in the heat. In their center a bird fetus, as if the food's processing has started to reverse.

I take a shot of vodka and feel it splash against the empty walls of my stomach. I hold the bottle out to Aimee and she takes a quick chug, tells me to hide it.

"Cam'll want some if he knows you have it," she says.

The alcohol's taking all my edges away and, for a second, I don't care.

"He ever explain what his problem was?" I ask, hearing a slur in my words already.

"No," she says. "I didn't ask him, either, though. You hungry?" She takes the bloodied pan off the stove. "We'll have to bury this really good," she says. "Cam's keeping that dog he knocked out, says he wants to train it to be our guard dog. The thing snapped at me twice today." She rolls up her plaid sleeve to show shallow gouges and red welts where teeth grazed her forearm.

Aimee's second attempt with the powdered eggs works. She cooks for all of us. We sit in the living room together, the way friends would.

"There's a show tonight," Trevor says. We hear of these things by watching for writing on dusty windows and handwritten posters pegged into the telephone poles with the stems of lost earrings and old staples.

I am craving a blackout period, something that will make me shudder out slight harmony, finality.

"Who's playing?" Aimee asks.

"Some band called Salt," Trevor says.

"Does it really matter who they are?" Brandy says. "It's not like there's anything else happening."

We make an exception for tonight and use some of the rainwater and soap to clean up. We don't tell anyone we're doing this, just lock ourselves in the bathroom—me, Aimee and Tara—and clean up as best we can.

Aimee gets in the tub first and we run wet cloths over her back, lather up the thin bar of soap. Tara's on her knees beside me and when she moves I can smell the soft yellow scent of her crotch. When she undresses I see that discharge has stuck to the back of her fly. The odour is like something between sex and recycled cardboard.

Our bodies are clean but our clothes are filthy—panties skid-marked and sleeves hard and dark at the pits. We try to hold onto our soapy skin as long as possible by rubbing patchouli under each arm and into our pubic hair. Tara even rubs it into the cap of her blue wig before pulling it on.

Tara picks up a pair of light blue cutoffs and rubs an extra drop onto the inseam where the denim's stained and stiff. She tops it with her black lace camisole, which has torn at the ribs and neckline.

There is no more orange lipstick, but Tara keeps the empty tube in her purse anyway, in case she's dreaming. To improvise, she wets a finger and dips it in a bowl of ashes on the floor. I resist the urge to lick the bowl after I see her doing this, my body trying to convince itself that anything could be food right now. Tara rubs the ash along her lips, tinting them charcoal, pulls her purse strap across her chest. It crushes against her small breasts.

"Ready to go?" she asks.

We ride, following Trevor and Cam. Brandy and Carrie are trailing behind us. We pass by an empty van that someone deco-rated by hand. VOLTRON RAINY NIGHTZ is spraypainted on one side. Tara brakes, touches these words as if they have power.

Cam and Trevor don't notice that we've stopped. Brandy and Carrie get ahead of us. They don't say anything as they go by.

"It's all right," Aimee says. "I know where they're going."

I pull out a few tabs of acid and ask them if they want one hit or two. We chase it all down with a shot of vodka.

The show's at an old strip club uptown. Someone's lit the place with candles around the sinks, baseboards, backs of the toi-lets. Two fingers on the mirror and Bloody Mary could be here.

Salt are already on the stage, getting ready for their first song. There are only ten other people here, not including the ones we live with. They all look vaguely familiar.

The singers take either side of the pole and it shimmers between them. I remember these girls, Jade and Leah. They used to be different people, had different identities. Jade was from a band called White Eagle and Leah from a band called Girl. Both groups lived in the same jam space, before The End came. They always threw the best parties.

I'd heard Jade and Leah both woke up one day with their hair turned white, all the way through, and they were both missing an eye—Leah her right and Jade her left. Their other band members were all in comas, flesh at their earlobes and inner elbows turning to cinders. I heard that they waited for seven nights for someone to wake up before moving the bodies outside.

Tonight they're doing an acoustic set, two girls spinning notes out of rusty strings and rigid bodies.

"You will live through this," they sing, but there's no conviction from the singers or the audience. We all remember it as an old lyric from a different time. We all subconsciously answer it with defiance.

It's my body and I'll die if I want to.

Cam comes up to Aimee with a double-dose of grayline as an apology for what happened earlier with the dog. "I thought I could teach him faster than it's taking," Cam says.

Aimee thanks him and takes a pill for herself, gives the other to me when he's not looking. It kicks in with the acid all at once and suddenly this club is an envelope that I am being stuffed into.

My chest constricts until I get outside, get some air. Light a cigarette and lean against the outside wall of the club.

The moon's low again. It feels like it's been full for days now, its cycle broken like everything else. It provides enough light to show the name of the club on the brick: Baby's, written in bright pink cursive.

The temperature plummets in the time it takes me to finish my smoke. It starts to snow. My cigarette hisses as it's extinguished by a heavy flake. We all came out tonight in bare arms. If the snow sticks, we might have to walk our bikes back.

I go inside to see if Aimee wants to get going. "They only have two more songs left," she says. "Let's go after that."

I don't want to stay but I sit down anyway. Tara's digging patterns into the tabletop with her nails: deep swirls and crosses. She catches me watching her and says, "I have to draw twenty of each symbol," she says, "or else."

"Or else what?" I ask, but her head's already back down, driven by whatever the drugs are dictating.

As Salt move through their last song, a girl slips onto the stage, starts twisting around the pole between them. Her hair hangs over one half of her face. She spins around the pole awkwardly on a broken heel. When she spins back around towards the room, her hair falls away from her face, uncovering a blank left side—no eye, no lips, no nostril.

"Shit," Aimee says when we get outside. "Why didn't you tell us it was snowing this bad?"

"I did," I tell her. "Not my fault you didn't listen."

The snow's already half a foot deep. Tara shivers. Her skin puckers from her ankles to her thighs. The girls of Salt step out behind us, trailed by the half-faced dancer. "Shit," Jade says at the snow.

"Where you girls headed?" Leah asks. Without waiting for an answer, she says, "We might just stay in the club. You're welcome to join us."

Tara's overheard whining, "I'm losing my buzz already."

"Don't worry," Jade says, her voice worn after tonight's singing. "We can fix you up—you got anything for us?"

Tara digs through her purse, spills its contents on the table. Jade picks through an amethyst ring, a hairbrush, an old set of keys. She takes the ring.

"I haven't had a new piece of jewelry in so, so long," she says.

"My first boyfriend gave that to me," Tara says, face straight, voice emotionless.

The girl with half a face tells me her name is Hamilton. I can smell her breath when she speaks. She hooks a leg over my lap.

"I didn't dream until I was sixteen," she says. "It started on the same night I stopped eating. I told a friend I was fat and she told me her sister's secret, that she'd lost seven pounds just by throwing up after dinner.

"When I stuck my fingernails down my throat and experienced life in reverse, that was when I really started living. I promised to never let food pass into me again, that all I'd ever crave would be the scrape of black nail polish on my tonsils.

"That first night, I dreamt of my possession, that the devil was in me and that he believed I could free him if I threw up hard enough. I always felt like I couldn't stand to be here for too long. Isn't that weird?"

"No," I tell her. "I know exactly what you mean."

Tara's fist slams against the table. "Ang!" she yells. "Watch this." She's got two pills in her palm and pours both of them out on her tongue at the same time. Hamilton's leg is still firm over my own but her eyes have glazed, body quiet and suddenly half-asleep.

Tara and I have special powers. I figure as much because no one else seems to hear Tara and I talking. Maybe it's because our lips aren't moving. Our voices have transcended their physical processes.

"It's quiet enough that we could lucid dream," Tara says. "Maybe that would bring back a piece of who I am, what I've forgotten."

"You think you've forgotten much?" I ask.

"Enough."

"Let's try to dream that the devil is here. Hamilton was talking about him earlier," I say.

"I think to do that we have to focus on the number thirty-four, which also adds up to the number seven, which is lucky for everyone but me," Tara says.

"Okay. And in this dream we're going to have, I am in an apartment, my own place. The devil's in the bathroom, rustling the shower curtain. I'm scared but I need to get in there because I have to get ready for work."

"Once," Tara says, "me and my friends tried to perform an exorcism. I can't remember why, but someone asked us to, this guy we kind of knew. So we went out to the woods and tried it, but it didn't work.

"That night, we all had the same dream: that we were back in the forest, trying to perform the exorcism again, except we lost all of our words. Like, we just couldn't remember how to talk anymore. I melted snow and turned it into holy water, hoping it would bring our words back, and it did. In my bag I had a prayer candle. Because it was something I'd bought for decoration and not for religious purposes, I didn't think it would work because it had the wrong intention behind it. I started the exorcism anyway. We all felt ready to finally have the devil gone. This was going to be a new start for us. But instead the devil only got stronger. We could hear him laughing in the trees. He thought it was funny that we were trying to turn things around when it was already way too late. We had no power because he already possessed us."

The next day the sun's blazing again and the snow's gone. We step cautiously to test the temperature and find it hot already, likely swinging back to being unbearably warm.

Tara corners Jade just as we're about to step out, wanting to pick up another dose, "to get through the day." Aimee and I wait outside.

"How addictive is this shit?" Aimee wonders.

"Probably depends on the person, just like anything else."

"Yeah," she says. "Maybe you're right. I'm not craving anything, are you?"

"I can feel the comedown about to get worse," I say. Actually, the more I think about it, the more I want some grayline, too. I don't mention this to Aimee.

There's food when we get back to the house, two raccoons and a small cat, their broken necks and bodies limp in Cam's and Trevor's hands. There's no blood on their hands or clothes, or on the animals. We don't ask how they killed these things. We don't breathe when we eat them, either, because we don't want to taste whatever disease they come with, or how close to decay they might have been when they died.

Cam's already thrown the innards and large bones to Taser, which is what he's named the canine beast now living with us. I ask if I can keep the pelts, for Shelley and Anadin. As a gift, an offering. Cam says I can only take them if I get rid of them right away. Says they'll attract animals if we hang onto them too long.

"Unless it gets cold again and stays cold," he says. That way the temperature could be enough for the rot to keep from setting in. I drape the pelts on a dead radiator for now, skin side up.

Everyone wants to bathe today. Me and Tara and Aimee don't mention we snuck baths last night already. We've all emptied our bowels since then and want another bath—you can only wipe yourself so clean with paper torn off telephone poles and old candy bar wrappers found under bushes. There's enough water to go around after last night's snow, though, so we go for it.

When it's my turn in the bathroom the sun against the window is yellow warmth. The water is lukewarm but I can pretend it's something luxurious.

Aimee's period pads are lined up in the windowsill, freshly washed again. We're all careful not to drop the soap in the tub or let it float in the water. Have to make it last as long as possible.

Despite the deep freeze overnight there are fruit flies in the air today. They mistake the soap for sustenance and float dead on their backs in the bath. I don't step out of the tub until I know there are no flies stuck to my body. Aimee offers up one of her t-shirts as a towel. The smell of her hair is embedded in the fabric. I wipe it over my waist, the backs of my arms, leaving traces of her all over me.

I wear Aimee's t-shirt out of the bathroom. It's just long enough to cover me to the tops of my thighs. In our bedroom, Tara's crouching on her mattress.

"I've got other pieces of the past I'd rather have back," she says. Her eyes are spinning, higher than last night. "But I'll take what I can get for now. I have to accept that because I accepted the name Valium and nothing was ever the same after that. Did I accept the demonic?" she asks.

My heart drops, even though the answer is no.

"This is a bonus round for me," she continues. "It all came to me just as I was cleaning up, which was also kind of like waking up. I'm so afraid to lose it again that I wrote it down. See?"

She points to a scrap of paper pinned to the wall with an animal's tiny bone:

Poetry was smeared on the mirror:
Who dreams in figures
1234 times plus 9 plus 4 equals
1111.
Big dreams in a miniature ghost world.

"I don't get it," I tell her.

"It doesn't matter," she says. "A few people have already told me about my aura today. They said it's glowing."

"Who told you that?" I ask.

"Oh, you missed them," she says. "They're already gone."

Later, I ask Cam who dropped by, but he says no one was here.

- 19 -
CULT OF SKULLS

Someone's been painting sugar skulls onto pieces of wood and nailing them to telephone poles. Their neon orange and green and pink grins bare at me on my way to the beach, bringing pelts to Shelley and Anadin. I can't tell if the skulls are meant to watch over us or if they're just watching.

When I left the house Tara was crawling, convinced she'd dropped a dose of grayline and that it was now wedged between the floorboards.

"Someone must have taken it then," she said when we told her we didn't lose any.

"Yeah, someone did," Cam said, and Tara glared up. "You."

She was on her feet her, then, lunging. He'd pushed her hard enough that she fell backwards, tailbone coming down against the hardwood. I slipped out then, not wanting anyone to notice where I was going, not even telling Aimee I was leaving for a while. There are some things I want to keep separate from the dirt and stress I live in.

There are also some things I want to get away from today. I've taken the house's moody energy with me in the form of a stomachache, which I'll leave on the beach, hopefully.

"I don't think that's the only reason you're hurting," Anadin tells me when I arrive. They've laid me down on their couch, which has sand between the cushions and springs poking into my back. Still, it's close enough to comfortable that I start to relax as Anadin rubs my stomach in small circles.

She looks into my eyes for a moment and nods, like she knows something I haven't told her. Can she see last night's hangover? Can she see I'm afraid of the cravings I'm starting to have? Any addiction before The End would have been hard enough to live through; now, though, without any reliable supplies or steady currencies, without any predictability of what grayline can really do, it's terrifying. But I don't say this out loud.

"When you hold the wrong things in, they spread their energy throughout your body," she says.

"It's true," Shelley says. "Whether you say it or not, your anger and anxiety and other emotions have to go somewhere if you don't let them out."

I've been giving myself and my stories away to the wrong people, for the wrong reasons. Even as I realize this, I know I won't stop.

Shelley and Anadin sit on the floor beside me while I run through every scrap of the past that I can with them:

—Me and Aimee, riding our bikes to the beach, this same beach, back when it was still alive. The backs of our arms were burning up in the midafternoon sun, but we didn't care. It felt good to be warm then.

—Too much time trying to forget pieces of ourselves that we'd ended up blanking out the wrong slates of awareness.

—Finally waiting for the confidence to admit to things I'd never wanted to acknowledge before. Just feeling ready to accept this was significant.

—A flash of Hunter's voice, something that once made me melt: "Before we'd ever talked I used to see you around and I'd want to scoop my hand into your liver, heart, lungs and pull whatever was left to the surface. I wanted to help you bring it all back. I could see it there, behind your eyes. You tried to wear it like apathy but I could see it was something else." Would I have done the same for him? Would he still feel that way now?

—When I moved back home from Vancouver, my mom, regardless of where I'd been the night before, would lay out red flannel shirts and wool socks for me on winter mornings while I was in the shower. I'd keep my hair wet and sit with her in the kitchen. She'd make grilled cheese and baked beans. I'd pour on too much ketchup. She'd sip black tea and watch me eat and we'd both pretend like nothing ever happened. The hardest thing to think of right now is that there was love in that house.

—In the den, TV on, stretched out on the couch with a blanket. Dad in his chair, reading the newspaper. I'd flip channels. It was Sunday morning. There was nothing on except gospel choirs and prayer sessions. We both fell asleep to hundreds of pairs of hands raised above us, praying, praising. Close to dreaming, I thought it was a sign—of safety. Of being saved. Of better things.

When I go over these points, I think of Hunter. Wish for an alternate outcome. Wish he was still here. Send him this message, in case he's listening: "Without you I need more air than I used to."

I pause, hang my head over the arm of the couch, away from Anadin and Shelley, to dry heave.

"Are you still full?" Anadin asks.

"From everything before?" Shelley adds.

"If you let one more thing stay inside of you, would you spill open?"

"Let it out," they both say together.

—I imagine that you are still here. When I am outside I think about the way the wind picked at your hair. I remember how you used to keep your hand on my neck to protect me from the cold. We used to hide in doorways in the rain, sharing cigarettes under your jacket. I'd hold the filter to your mouth and you'd kiss the palm of my hand to thank me.

Shelley and Anadin hold up the pelts, which I couldn't keep from rotting after all. The skin-side of the hides is blackening at the edges. The smell is something like the oldest tooth in a bad mouth. Shelley and Anadin have admiration for the pelts anyway.

"We can work with them," Shelley says.

"But first, we still have to work with you," Anadin says.

"I thought we were done," I say.

There could be love *here*, in this house, too. If I find a way to keep this beach house all for myself, protect it from the rest of what my life has become.

Outside, in the light, I see that one of Anadin's eyes has turned husky blue, a contrast against its original deep brown.

Chunks of her hair have gone white, almost translucent, streaks like underwater tentacles.

"Light a cigarette," she says. "It's a compromise. We'll cleanse by fire."

Shelley speaks: "There are old power lines, below the earth. They've gone tentative, but are still sending us signals. Visions. We see one for you, Ang, but it's not the right time to tell you."

"Is the vision just for me, or for my friends, too?"

"Just for you," Shelley says. "Just for you."

Anadin speaks: "This city's turning into a cult of skulls. You must have seen them on your way here."

Shelley chants, weaves these words as subtext. The skull: a mythology. Sacred to luck. Flesh and soul and intellect. Protector of death. Resurrection. Captivate. Calaveras. Day of the Dead. Skulls that were considered lucky. Dead dolls with skulls for heads. Empty eye sockets tattooed to inner arms. That luck isn't here anymore. There is nothing demonic, nothing divine here. Only everything in between: ghosts and raw nerves and miles of despair. Memento mori. Gothic disaffection.

Anadin speaks: "The skulls signal that the swing of the pendulum is starting to slow, stop. You will start to dream. It will be dark inside those dreams. Darker than the ones you know now, and full of predators. Things that grab at ankles, hands up your shirt. When you wake in the morning you'll want to hear that someone still knows you, remembers who you were before. But sometimes it feels like there are just so many words on top of words that they're all backed up. Sometimes all you can do is skim off the surface instead of pulling from the bottom of the pile, where the real words got buried."

They walk me down the beach and bend me over behind a big rock. I feel my insides rise right away. "I can't handle being sick anymore," I tell them.

"You'll make it through," they say, as the first wave comes up. I throw up a tube of lipstick. The cap comes off and the smear of colour inside is burnt orange. They rub my back through another contraction—out comes an empty charm bracelet. I pant through the pain my chest. My head swims again and out comes a trail of charms. They scatter across the sand. A cramp crosses my entire abdomen, from the right side to the left. I have to get on all fours for this one. Shelley and Anadin hang on to my shoulders now, brush hair back from my face as I feel fur and bone pass the wrong way over my tongue. The snout of a raccoon falls out, fur partially torn from the bone, a row of teeth and broken whiskers hanging on.

I could suffocate, can't catch my breath. "Breathe through it," Anadin says, as though she knows what I'm feeling without being able to tell her.

I get a hold of a decent inhalation and let it out slowly. The pain leaves me. No cramps, no stomachache. I breathe in again to make sure the absence is real. It is.

The sun feels good, makes me want to stay out of the house. I swing by to see if Aimee and Tara want to stay out with me but they're not around when I get there. I head back out alone again and ride.

There's a park down the street from here, but when I pull closer I find a group of men there. Their heads swing in my direction, as if they've caught my scent. I put a hand over the knife in my pocket, just needing the reassurance it's there. I keep riding.

"You still hanging around here?" This is the question that makes me jump at the Mission, but the voice makes me stay; it's too familiar.

Tooth comes out from under the stage, walks towards me. I haven't heard anything about the Shit Kitten guys since their show at the brick factory.

We're in each other's arms. "What are you doing here?" I ask.

"Thinking about doing another show," he says. "It'll probably be our last."

"Why?"

He tells me that the skulls going up around town are a marker of the final days for the city. "You know how the electricity still sometimes buzzes on? Well, it's really going to be over soon. Next time it goes off, it's off for good."

Tooth tells me there's a skull at the city's center where everyone's heart used to beat from. In its place now is a skull on a hypnotist's spiral, in the center of its forehead an all-seeing eye in a pyramid.

"This whole place is a public altar, all of it," he says. "The skulls are feeding off whatever's left of this city's spiritual essence. They're feeding off whoever is still out there."

Tooth tells me of sepulchral lamps below the subway, where the train tunnels have been turned into catacombs. At least that's what he heard. With bands, the myth is always better than the reality. I listen anyway, choose to believe that anyone not disappeared, only dead, has been thrown into piles below the streets. By who, exactly, he's not sure.

"When this city was alive you could feel the trains pulling in under your feet," he says. "If you were standing in the right place at the right time you could feel the city shudder with the thrill of steel and sparking tracks as the trains wormed through it."

It's true. There was magic here.

"There still is," he says.

Except now the city squeezes out hollowed groans of gaping skulls, the agonized wind tunnels of a subterranean spirit world. This will be the urban legend for the apocalyptic generation, that any energy left is being funneled below. The dead need a light at the end of their tunnel and they are going to use ours to get it. Now, with every step we take, we will do it with the dead in mind, imagine that their mouths are hanging long and low in mock horror as they send shivers through us all.

"How do you even know that you can be heard over a death chant?" I ask.

"Guess we'll find out at the show, won't we?" Tooth says.

Cam's dog is in the house. At least that's what I'm thinking as I pull into the driveway. The sun's going down, fast. There are a few candles already lit in the windows.

The howling follows me to the mudroom at the back. I don't know why I'm running inside when I feel like I should be running back out to the street, but here I am anyway.

I get through the kitchen and that's when the sound changes enough to know it's not Taser. It's a girl. My head runs through the possibilities, of course goes to Aimee and Tara first.

Cam and Trevor and Brandy are in the living room, circled around Carrie, who's on the floor. Someone's shoved the coffee table off to the side. Or maybe that's where it's been since Cam shoved Tara across the room earlier.

Everyone's talking in quick whispers, tones blended with fear and urgency and tepid reassurance. I'm thinking I should offer to help in some way but don't even know what's going on, so I keep a few steps back, in case they think I'm intruding. Maybe I *am* intruding.

Carrie's in her leather jacket and lace bra, her usual wear. Someone's put a blanket beneath her.

Brandy meets my eyes. "Is she sick?" I ask.

"I don't know," she says. Her eyebrows unite in worry.

Carrie's covered in sweat. Brandy breaks my gaze to get Carrie's jacket off. I've never seen her without it before, not even on the hottest days. Her arms are a network of tattoos she's kept hidden: an anatomical heart, a skull, a spider web on her elbow. Things Hunter would have sneered at and called typical. I see a pentagram on her bicep, a row of names and dates, a black and white portrait of a woman with long dark hair.

Carrie moans, arches her back. Brandy looks at me again.

"She just collapsed and when she woke up she couldn't talk," she says.

Carrie's nose starts to bleed. We all just stand there and stare. She moans again, looks close to tears. I go upstairs and lie down, plug my ears as another wave of Carrie's pain surges through the house.

I fall asleep and dream of a couple. The girl is small but dominant. Decisive. She wears blue eyeliner and has a beauty mark on her lower right cheek. She would have been popular in high school.

The man is tall, built. A little bit older than us. Also dominant, but not towards her. They have chosen me as their third and their surrogate. I will carry their child, and the child will be a wolf.

It's not the man who has sex with me. He just watches, makes sure we're doing it right.

The girl is a shapeshifter. Her animal self is a male dog, half wolf. They expect that I will shapeshift, too. They know something about me that I don't, and even though I trust their conviction I doubt that I will be able to change.

The girl mounts me as a human, in the missionary position. As she pumps into me her body starts to change. The in-between of her face is a horror movie vampire, half transformed into its creature state. Her forehead is ridged and her shoulders are bulked.

She pushes her fingers hard into my collarbone. It hurts so much I expect something to break.

"You should be changing by now," she says. "This might help your shoulders come forward."

I know that whether I change or not, the story will end in the same way: I will become pregnant and birth a wolf. I will love it, but it will never be mine.

I wake up. The sun's completely gone down now. Aimee must have come in after I fell asleep because she's in bed beside me, breathing evenly. Downstairs, Carrie is still gasping, whimpering. I can hear her through the floor.

In the candlelight of the living room Carrie is blue-white, eyes wide, protruding. Brandy wipes foam from her friend's mouth. Trevor holds a cloth to Carrie's forehead as her hips buck up off the mattress. Her body slumps beneath his touch and a puff of unsettled dust rises from below her.

Carrie pulls at her pants, says it's too hot to keep them on. Cam is in the corner, keeping his distance. He doesn't make a move to help so I get down at Carrie's ankles and pull.

There's blood between her legs, leaking through the crotch of her panties. It starts as a slow pool before whooshing out, intestines, liver, kidneys, a stew of worms slick along the inside of Carrie's thighs. Brandy draws a sharp breath and puts a hand to her friend's forehead, intended to comfort. Below her touch, something bulges at Carrie's temples. Her scalp sheds its hair and, newly bald, shines with swelter.

Carrie's eyes shut, seal. Her temples stretch to breaking—on the sides of her head emerge new eyes, bulging and wide. She screams and her voice crescendos from woman to baby. Her hand comes up, reaching, but her fingers are stumps, fist a nub, arm shrinking up into the shoulder socket.

"Oh my God," Brandy says, "her legs. Look at her legs." In seconds they've been sucked up, too, until Carrie's nothing but the block of a body, a deep purple torso and head, no neck, no body cavities. Her cry weakens over a stopping heart as my body does something that feels like fainting.

When I open my eyes again, I am in bed. The sun's burning low and orange in the sky, right beside an amber moon the colour of a cat's eye. I am the only one still in bed. I must have been asleep for hours. Or unconscious. I didn't even hear anyone get up.

I listen for the drop or scrape of something heavy on the floor: a boot or an empty bottle. I listen for a voice, a shout, but I get nothing back.

I get up and reach for a cigarette. Down to my last two. I wonder if Aimee and Tara are getting low on theirs. It'll be a good excuse to get out of here.

Maybe I should just not come back. This house, it's not good for any of us.

Aimee and Tara are in the bathroom, sitting on the edge of the dry bathtub. Tara's got her arms wrapped around herself like she's trying to keep warm. I can count every bone in her body from here.

Aimee's rushing a smoke to her mouth, taking two drags at a time like she can't get enough in. They're so focused on themselves that it takes a few seconds before they notice I'm here.

"You know what happened last night," Aimee says. Her left knee bounces. Every jolt knocks away the ash off the end of her cigarette.

"Yeah." I take a final drag off my own and put it out in the sink. Aimee offers her cigarette to me. The filter is wet with her spit.

"The body's gone, you know," Tara says. "Don't know where they went with it, but they didn't want it around. Cam's worried it might contaminate the house." There's the usual gravel in Tara's

voice but it's got a childish tone mixed in today, nerves tightening all the way through to the vocal chords.

"They all left a couple hours ago," Aimee says.

"Are they coming back?" I ask.

"They said they weren't sure," Tara says.

20

3LINK

Blink and an hour passes. There's a glass of vodka, filled to the top, at my lips. I swallow and the liquid sticks in my throat like a tentative syllable, strong enough to bring the whole building down. Blink and I'm a blank slate of recall, lips slightly bruised. A taste of new territory in the mouth.

This sense of travel, this transcendence of time-space-moments, is what Tooth would say is the result of disrupting the universe. I told him I'm not really supposed to be alive right now and he said, "That makes more sense than anything I've ever heard."

I am one of a handful of people still at the Mission. Shit Kitten played a set but I only know it happened because Aimee keeps telling me it's already done. Blink and you'll miss everything.

Four out of ten people are staring right at me. Total mess. I lose my balance and fall forward, knock an empty bottle into someone's lap on the other side of the booth. I apologize but the two girls across from me pretend I'm not there.

Get outside and the sun is still out. Streets empty, except for Tooth, sitting on the corner, smoke in hand.

"Hey," he says. I hang onto the telephone pole on my way over to him.

"So that's it?" I ask. "Is it all over?"

"I'm thinking of going to Montreal," he says. "We all are. We heard things aren't as bad there yet. Heard there are places we could stay, people who can help us out."

The road is radiating heat. It smells like unwashed hair. I find a cigarette on the ground, barely smoked. Pick it up and light it.

"You better say goodbye to me before you go," I say.

"Don't worry," Tooth says. "I'll let you know."

Cam and Trevor have come back to the house but Brandy is gone. We don't ask where she went, but assume we won't see her again. Maybe she's walking home like she always wanted to.

With fewer people around there are fewer sounds to cover up the hauntings. Today the ghost upstairs is active, but I am the only one listening and she knows it. She likes to be asked questions but says she's sad that no one ever wants to ask her anything. Little girl ghost. Ask her what she feels and she'll tell you about the cold between her legs, how it twists and licks around the tops of her thighs, its tongue a trunk of steel, simultaneous mix of tease and dread.

Ask her about the noise, all day, all night sometimes. She knows we don't like to listen to her. She says she listens to us talking and moving and waits for a break in everything so she can move and talk, too.

Ask her what she's built like and she'll say, "Claws in my toes, long black beaks and moons in my fingernails. Bird species underside."

Listen and she'll say, "This is how I play." And then scratch—SCRRRAAATCH—as urgent as a dog at a screen door. Her voice is a whisper-growl, a half-squeal that's caught in the black tar drips down the back of an old throat.

Ask her how she died and she'll say she doesn't remember.

I can't sleep right now, so I think of it for her. I wait for a transformation to hit me. Count to sixty but get nothing. My buzz—a mix of hard liquor and whatever anyone would give me last night—is finally starting to wear off. I should be passed out. I must have eaten some speed at one point.

A hangover hits me at the same rate of my declining euphoria. I'm suddenly at the bathroom sink, dry-heaving until my nausea's disrupted by something grabbing at my feet.

My body believes there is only a sliver of reality here. I wonder how much of it shows, and if I am beginning to forget what connected my brain to these bones before I was ever able to come together at all.

Back in bed I try to remember why I am still here. A shadow thought pulls at a memory that feels like regret but scrambles to get the thread between its teeth. My head spins but I still can't sleep so I think of Hunter: black leather and the ocean and a calloused fingertip rubbing my softest skin. I think of incongruent meetings and the rhythm of our pushing and pulling. I think of how I knew he would always be in my head, but never imagined there'd be a day when he was nowhere else.

I'm interrupted by choking sounds. Gagging. The distortion of Tara's voice box. She's in her own withdrawal and it's too much for my ears. I've heard enough, can't take in any more resonance.

"Can you hear them?" The little girl ghost is still above me, reaching out, but I bet she feels nothing. When she gets inside me she'll know I'm empty, the dead's equivalent of avoiding eye contact.

I can tell that today is one of those days where no moment will ease into the next. It will all just slam together. I know this because Aimee and I go from being in bed to being out the door, doing a run for Tara. We left her sick on the floor, begging.

Okay, so we aren't just going for Tara. We're going for ourselves, too. But when someone's kicking worse than you it's easy to disguise your habits as charity.

Three blocks away we see a small group of people.

"I wonder who that is?" Aimee asks, as though we should know everyone.

There are four guys and a girl. The girl raises her hands, bends deep and cartwheels into the road. Her body curves as her legs flip. She lands on her ass.

She pulls herself together, positions her hands to push off the asphalt. None of the guys with her offer to help. She's about to stand and then stops, feeling something beneath a pile of debris on the road. Out comes a shard of foggy glass, as long and crooked as a wizard's finger.

"Look what I found!" she yells, legs taking off as she leaps up, runs towards the next block and vaults a newspaper box. There's still a newspaper inside.

"Let's grab that," Aimee says. "We can use it for a fire."

We're coming up just behind the group now. The girl stabs the air, spins and kicks at an imaginary opponent before she sees us riding up.

"You wanna have a sword fight?" she asks, stabbing the air between her and us. We just laugh, shake our heads no, even though I wish we could.

"No," she says, her voice lower now. "No, I know what you want, though. I can read it on you. You're looking for grayline," she says, pointing a scabbed finger at us.

"Lucky guess," Aimee says.

"You know who has the best?" the girl asks.

We follow her directions to a house not far up the road. We knock on the door and ask for Chris. He answers wearing only boxer shorts stiff at the front with sticky-dry stains.

He looks from me to Aimee, Aimee to me, me to Aimee again. "Hmm," he says, "which one will I choose first?" His eyes dart over each of us one more time and then he smiles and points to Aimee. "You," he says. "You come with me."

Fair enough. I know what I look like: stringy hair so greasy it's gone from white-blonde to sandy beige. Cheeks sunken, accenting my skull. I stopped wearing a bra because there's nothing for it to hold anymore. Everything has fallen away from me, like it always has.

I sit in the hallway outside Chris' bedroom, where he told me to wait. He hasn't shut the door all the way and I can hear him in there:

"The other week, I stopped outside a store I used to go to all the time. The front windows had been smashed out, or maybe they just fell apart. I wanted to look inside but knew there was nothing left. A few feet away there was a body in the road. I'd never seen a dead body before. I haven't seen many around, surprisingly. Have you? Anyway, there were animals around it, eating. I didn't want to go near it but I couldn't stop myself, either, so I went over and it was the body of a little kid. The skin was green and grey. It was hard to tell if it had been a boy or a girl, but from the clothes I'd say it was a boy. There were dogs and a cat and a raccoon all in there, eating at the neck and belly, all the soft spaces. The animals didn't even run when they saw me. It's like they know they have all the power now.

"Anyway," he says, "I'm so glad you're here because I can't stop thinking about it. I really had to tell someone and you're that person. Just you, just now."

When you talk about something, you're letting it go. Keep it in and it seals itself inside of you. The longer it's in there, the deeper it gets. But what happens to the person you tell it to? Does it move on to go live with them? Will Chris' stories live with us after we leave here?

I already want to go and I've just gotten into bed with him. He's different from Mike. Aggressive. His leg is over top of mine, applying too much pressure. Like he's trying to keep me in place.

He's pressing up hard against my butt and I can feel it's making him grow. He asks me to tell him something. I don't want to but I don't want to have to lie here for longer than I need to, either. Might as well as just do what he wants.

"I feel like I have to—"

I don't get the rest of my sentence out before his hand cups a nub that used to be of one of my breasts. He massages it with a massive, heavy grip, and talks:

"How did I think I would even live through this?" he asks. "There are stories. I've heard them from other people who've come here to pick up. One girl told me she was running out of her neighbourhood the night of the big fires when a woman's body dropped right beside her. At first she thought the woman had a heart attack or something but no, she'd been hit on the head with a rock. There was a guy standing right there with the rock still in his hand, ready to bring it down again.

"But you know what the girl remembers about that? Not what the guy looked like, or if anyone stopped to do anything. No, she remembers that there was still fat in this woman's face and around her middle. It would have been gone in another week or two had she lived, of course."

None of us expected to have to know what to do for this long, on our own. We never knew we'd have to pick through other people's stories while they picked at us, just so that we could pick up.

I try to convince myself that this is easier than I expected, staying here beside Chris. The promise that the day holds is that I'll soon be wrapping myself around the floor, and that's enough to get me through this. I will get through this.

We don't make it out of Chris's house. At least not right away. When you can swallow things that'll take away whatever heaviness you have left you bring weakness to all you want to forget. You realize this when you're high but when you're sober you can't get that feeling back. You remember having it, and you remember the knowledge it gave, but you can't remember how to access it under your own will.

Open hands. That's what I wake up to, after falling asleep beside Chris. Mistake Number One right there. He runs his hands, spread flat and wide, over my ass, my stomach. He glides over my bellybutton and I flutter inside. *I could come right now*, I think, surprised that my body is still capable of reacting this way.

I scream at myself but keep it all in my head. Disgusted by what my hips are begging for, disgusted by Chris's touch. Another second and I might have screamed outside of myself, but voices barge through the front door.

Chris jumps out of bed. "You and your friend can stick around if you want."

If you can start drinking and drugging as soon as you're awake, split a dusty bottle of sour wine with some girl you've just met, you can trick yourself into thinking things aren't so bad. Get enough of a buzz and the house you're in, no matter how much its walls creep on you, can start to feel okay, like you can at least relax here. The dirt—and we're talking about a different kind of dirt than the usual film that covers everyone's skin now—starts to dissipate, drift away. You can lie to yourself that you're cleaner now than when you started. You can ignore what you know: that later tonight, or tomorrow, you'll have never wished for a shower so badly before.

I get into a chugging contest with some girl named Sarah. Says she knows Chris but doesn't say they're friends. The wine that came with her and two other guys was lifted from some basement of a house they broke into along the way.

I win the competition but it's Sarah who's stumbling around the room now, telling everyone, "You're fucked out of your mind!"

The guys are laughing but me and Aimee just look at each other. I want to leave, but before I get the words out to say so a guy with long brown hair and a beard to match walks over with an open hand and says, "This will help you girls." It's more grayline. We pop the pills in our mouths and this guy sits down, talks. His mouth moves but his lips are shooting blanks.

Aimee shakes his hand, makes a deal I'm deaf to. He holds his hand out to me and I take it but can't even say my name because my face is a seizure of light and shade, flicking on and off, a rhythm I can't catch up to.

The sun's grim in the window and everyone's hiding from it in the shadows until Chris pulls the curtains shut. The fluorescent flicker hits the whole room and that's when I know I'm really tripping because there is no electricity today.

Sarah stops and starts, goes from dancing to talking in thirty-second intervals, her movements disjointed by the in-out-in of bright to black.

I need some air. I have to hold onto the arm of the couch to get up off the floor. A voice—Aimee's, I'm guessing—is trying to break through the density around my skull, but its steady fall of consonants and vowels bump softly against my earlobes and can't get far enough inside to be heard. A hand buffets my calf but I have to keep moving towards the door.

The on-and-off light follows me through the hallway. It falls around the face of someone who's just walked in: a guy with thin, stringy hair that's still holding onto fading blue dye.

It's his words that penetrate. "You going outside?"

He reaches for the door handle. My brain tells my head to nod but the body doesn't get the signal. He keeps his hand where it is.

"You're not leaving, right? Just going outside?" That he knows this must mean he has ESP.

I reach for the handle and his other hand comes up to stop me. His hand is warm. I want to hold it. I want to be held. Not by Mike or Chris. Not for a transaction but for comfort.

I hold onto this guy's hand and try to smile. Maybe he'll come outside with me.

"You have a cigarette?" he asks. This time my brain and body are back together and I nod.

"Yes."

"K," he says. "But let's go out back. Chris doesn't like people hanging out at the front. Besides, it's dangerous."

He hooks his fingers through my belt loops and yanks me to him, catches me with his mouth. His fingers are fast, already kneading the crotch of my shorts, working the fly. He sticks two fingers inside of me and I know I've soaked him. I moan and push against him, a signal to increase the pressure.

I reach for his zipper. He gets me up on the railing of the deck. He's standing on my shorts. My panties are still on, pushed to the side. "I like the way you smell," he says when I move to take them off.

He slides into me and lifts me up. My legs wrap around his back. He's got a ring through his eyebrow. The piercing looks fresh, or infected. The red of the swelling overwhelms the silver jewelry. I reach for his face, careful not to get too close to the inflamed loop. We've barely kissed and he's already finished. I grind myself into his pubic hair to tell him I want more but he's already lifting me away, putting me back down.

It's the first time I'm noticing how unfocused his eyes are. He must be as fucked up as I am.

"I didn't even get your name when I came in," he says, zipping up his jeans.

"I don't care," I tell him.

Back inside, Sarah's in the middle of the living room, dancing with her eyes closed. It's just her and Aimee and the guy with the beard left.

"Where's everyone else?" I ask.

"Upstairs," Aimee says. There's a needle in her voice. "You've been gone forever."

"I just went outside for a minute," I tell her.

"More like an hour," Aimee says.

Sarah stumbles out of step. I fall for the distraction. There is a stereo here but nothing to power it. The music is all coming from her, every movement curving into the next, expelling beats and extending rhythms. Her eyes stay shut the entire time, even when she loses her balance.

"You ready to go yet?" Aimee asks.

I think of things I could have today, and things I didn't know I've been wanting: skin on skin, arms around me when I sleep, a wet spot in my pubic hair.

I turn for the guy with the blue hair. For a look, maybe, a sign that I should stay, but he's not around. Probably went upstairs to look for Chris. Everyone's here for the same reason we are: to get high. I feel rejected anyway.

I nod, keeping my eyes on my boots. "Yeah," I say to Aimee. "We can go."

Back outside, the sun's starting to go down. "At least we'll get back before it's dark," Aimee says.

Tara's asleep in the closet again. We call her, watch her twitch into wakefulness.

"You're back!" She jumps up and onto my bed. "What'd you bring me?"

I look at Aimee and feel even worse when I see that her face looks as sick as I suddenly feel.

"Fuck." The word comes out of me before I have time to even feel it working its way up, before I have any notice that it's about to give us away.

Tara's face is melting with the slack of a lack of pills. Her jaw twists like something loosely oiled, a door about to fall off a hinge. Her neck hits an ugly angle. "You didn't bring anything back, did you?" she says, and I cover a groan with a nervous laugh.

"Ang," Tara says, laying a hand on my arm, flexing her fingers to remind me of the long nails at the end of each of them. "Ang," she says again, her voice pulling my heart into my throat.

My jaw absorbs all the tension. It's so tight I wonder if I'll be able to speak.

A dogfight rumbles up from the street. We're three floors up but it sounds like they're in the room with us, growls coming from the core. We don't have to see their teeth to know what they look like. The sounds alone are more colour than we've seen in a month.

I am tired. The exhaustion envelops me, takes me over. My head sinks to shoulder level and I rub my eyes which have gone sandpaper dry, as thirsty as my throat. The whole day's passed by and I haven't had any water. Any energy I've been running on today is just psychedelic residue.

Face to face on the floor, Tara fingers the swelling above my cheeks. Sickness and fluids have all congealed in under-eye bags, where they wait to be flushed out.

I lie to Tara: "I'm not as bad as I look."

She slides forward until her face is almost touching mine, close enough that when she speaks her words trip across the bridge of my nose. She looks at me like she's been in my head for too long.

"I can't remember if you're still who I expected you to be," she says as I begin to fall asleep.

I wake up. It's dark but the moon has gone the bright white of a bare bulb, cold enough to burn.

Tara is still up. She's playing around with a long black evening glove, pulling it up to her elbow and then rolling it back down. Something silk and vintage, the lost half of a pair.

"You're not tired?" I ask, so tired myself that I'm still on the floor. I pull myself onto my mattress and feel an ache starting in my neck from sleeping on the hardwood.

"I'm waiting for Aimee," she says.

"What for?" I ask.

"She went back out."

"Back out where?"

"Back to wherever you guys got that grayline earlier," she says. "I told her I really needed some and she went out to get it. Felt bad that you forgot earlier."

"She went alone?" I ask.

"Yeah."

I pretend to fall asleep but really I'm pretending to be somewhere else. In a club. Brief touches on a crowded dancefloor, colliding slightly with curving bodies, cold bottles brushing the backs of my arms.

I fall asleep for real and dream that Tara's been stashing pills, holding out on us. I dream that she's had pills crawling down her throat all night because she's so afraid of dipping below the highest high.

In my dream she's smoking a joint, still admiring her silk glove as she shows off a French inhale. She tells me that people have been catching narcolepsy, that it's been going around lately, turned into a mutant pollution. "Anything can happen if you let your head dip below your chin."

In my dream I wish, distinctly, for Tara to be right in her diagnosis, to give me something that will keep me asleep as often as possible.

21

WE ALL HAVE STORIES LIKE THAT

Aimee's leg stretches towards me. I roll down her torn fishnets, shredded at the knees to match the skin below. Before now, hers was the only pair still perfectly intact. Parts of the stockings stick to the dried blood on her leg. I'm careful in those spots not to pull at a wound.

Aimee sticks a hand out to help me, but all it can do is shake. I stick a cigarette in her fingers and tell her, "It's okay, I got it."

Aimee disguises a sob with the drag of the smoke. If she starts crying again, I might, too. At least her chest isn't heaving like it was when she first got here. She'd run through the house, torn up the stairs and woken me up before she even got to the bedroom. Her face purple streaks on her cheeks, impossible blotches of what I first thought was mascara. It was really just her head leaking pigments.

She held her t-shirt together with one hand. Below her grasp, deep red flashed across her chest for a beat. "Aimee," I said, "come here. What happened?" Her shirt was almost ripped in half, torn down to her navel. Trembling knuckles held the two flaps of fabric together.

Now Aimee takes a sharp pull on the cigarette as I dab at the scrapes with a damp cloth. Black grit peppers the pink pulp of her knees where she fell, trying to get away. We speak in whispers, listening for the rest of the house. "I just don't want to see Cam," she'd said when I got her into the bathroom. "I shouldn't have gone alone. He'll ask why I did. He'll tell me I made a mistake." A pause, and then: "I don't want to tell him what happened."

Aimee breathes hard through the pain again and I soften my voice for her and say "sorry" and "it's okay" and "I'm almost done." We find a rhythm between her breath and my words, a horrible little chant that fills the bathroom that somehow seems too small with both of us in it, sharing space with last night's shadow that's followed Aimee back here.

I've filled the tub with rainwater. Cam gave me a look when he saw me carrying buckets upstairs. I shot him one back to keep him from asking questions. Besides, the sky looks like it's darkening, getting heavy with more water to let loose on us. We'll be fine if it rains within another day.

I joke to Aimee to close her eyes and pretend the water's steaming, pretend the room is filled with the pink scent of bubble bath. Channel decadence.

I unzip the back of her skirt. It falls around her ankles. There's a hard, dark blemish of blood gone brown at the back of it and her panties are missing. Or maybe she wasn't wearing any. I don't ask. Just kick the skirt behind me before she sees the stain.

Aimee holds my hand as she steps into the tub. The heel of her palm is rough where the skin caught the pavement. She doesn't flinch this time.

I run water over her back, ignore the fruit flies that are already skirting the bath's surface. I pick them out as I can so they don't stick to Aimee or her open sores. We continue our quiet chant. Aimee's breaks up with faltering sobs again. I maintain the softer chorus.

Tara has smoothed the blankets over Aimee's bed and laid out an oversized t-shirt for her to wear. It's not anything that belongs to us, must have been left behind by one of the girls, or taken from Cam or Trevor. I bring it to my face, smell for dust or odour, any trace of potential infliction. It's as clean as anything here can be. I help Aimee slide into it, feel guilty for noticing that she still has curves in certain places.

Tara takes a brush to Aimee's hair, starts working her way through. We stop talking. We've said enough before, at other times, when this happened to other girls we knew, or girls we'd heard of. At parties, or in their bedrooms. With boys they knew, boys they trusted, boys they'd just met. Except then there were more friends to call. There were mothers, sisters. There were hot showers and clean clothes. There were familiar kitchen tables and beds that had never belonged to the dead.

Aimee's already trying to look like she doesn't give a fuck. Like everything is fine and it's just another night. "This one might be the last," she says, mickey in hand, but we've all said that before.

"Doesn't mean it's not true this time," Tara says, stealing my thoughts. We knock bottles together and each take a shot of warm rye. At least Aimee still got out of Chris's with what she'd gone in there for.

We don't mention last night, though. We don't look at the bruise rising on Aimee's left cheekbone. We don't let the scab on her chin distract our eyes. We don't act like there's anything different in the way she lowers herself to sit, carefully, slowly, bracing for pain.

We get drunk while we get dressed for Shit Kitten's going away party. Rattail came by earlier to invite us. I pull on my gold panties because it's a special occasion. The elastic stings as it hugs a blister on my hip. I don't remember how it got there.

"Probably from sleeping on the floor," Tara offers. Or from rubbing up against that guy I met yesterday. Doesn't matter. Another shot and the pain will be gone.

Shit Kitten have been living in a place called the Heebie Jeebies house. It's had that name as long as anyone can remember. Haunted, just like everything else in this city these days.

The plaque outside says it was built in 1858. Someone's scratched into it, though, generations of squatters and punks and hobos making their mark, leaving their names and messages carved into the metal so others could find them here. Some of the names are barely legible in the brass which has turned orange, green, turquoise. A new history with every fresh dig and nick and now it's all for nothing; it only means something if someone's here to see it.

The word SLAUGHTERHOUSE is spraypainted on the living room wall. Heebie Jeebies house was first a home, then a slaughterhouse, then a rooming house, then abandoned. It has been a squat ever since and remains so today. A building for transients and transience.

Tooth squatted here for a while before The End. At least this is the story he's telling me now, beside me on the floor. He pushes a dose of grayline into my palm when no one's looking and asks, "You want to hear something crazy?"

His eyes are blue. If he were to live to be older, the lines around them would be deep but friendly. He's kept his hair short, the ends uneven where he's cut them with a knife.

He's smiling, waiting for me to answer.

"Yeah," I tell him. "I want to hear something crazy."

So he says there's something in this house called the Love Object. It lives in the walls. At night they can hear it dragging its hind legs, its spirit immolated to the room's past. Overtaken by heartworm, it sags so heavily its crawls drag like wrought iron on a raw wood floor. He says at night sometimes they hear groaning animals. He's heard hooves clop on the floorboards. He says when he was squatting here a few years back, someone tried to put carpet down once, when the noise was particularly bad. The next day, though, someone was cutting lines of cocaine and knocked it all onto the floor by accident, lost all the coke in the carpet fibers so it was back to bare floors after that. He says there was a girl here around that same time who'd locked herself in one of the rooms and slit her wrists. Two days passed before anyone thought to break the door down.

"And you were here for that?" I ask.

"Yeah, I was living here, but I was in Buffalo, playing a show when that happened. I helped break into the room when I got back, though."

"Did you know her?"

"Yeah, I knew her. She was cool. Quiet, kind of."

"Do you think you could have stopped her?"

"I don't know," he says. "I tried not to think about that too much after it happened."

"Do you think it had something to do with the house?" I ask.

"Yeah, actually," he says. "Bad energy. I've heard of stuff like that getting to people." He pauses to chug from a bottle. "I mean, I'd like to think that I could have helped that girl, but I don't know. Can you ever really stop anyone who really wants to die?"

"If they really want to die, and you stop them anyway, they kill themselves in other ways," I say. "But if they want to be saved, then yeah, you can stop them." As I say this, I still don't know which of these is true for me.

Tooth has a joint between his lips and an arm around my shoulder. I think of the first time I was in a car with Hunter. He was driving and put his arm around the headrest of my seat to back up out of a driveway. I knew he was just doing what he had to do but I still wanted to believe there was meaning in that gesture, that it was a way for him to get closer to me.

Tooth says it feels like I'm holding him upright and I wonder if he's thinking of anyone else right now. I can't remember ever seeing him with a girlfriend. I don't know if he has family, if he has a sister or a brother. I only ever saw him with the rest of his band, or with people from the Mission.

He pulls on the joint and hands it to me. We don't need to channel decadence anymore tonight because it's all right here, the most booze and drugs we'll probably ever see again. I take a deep drag and Tooth moves into me, closer. The bottle is still three-quarters full. It jostles between us, heavy and unpredictable. Fire water. Something scuttles in the wall behind us, teasing our tailbones, waiting to suck us dry.

Tooth wants to suck me dry. His tongue is a strawberry and I take it into my mouth all at once. My jaw pops. Tooth's fingers are up the front of my cutoffs, fingering the gold spandex beneath.

"*I was going to get everything right . . .*" a voice sings out over a rushing chord. The whole room stops. Music has always commanded us, but now that it only occupies the in-between of our lives instead of the everyday it grabs us even harder. Rattail's got the room now, just he and an acoustic guitar, his voice filling us.

Tara appears beside me. "I didn't know anyone was going to play tonight." Her words are too close together. I can tell she's shitfaced.

A girl with golden hair down to her waist starts crying. I remember her face. She's someone I used to see around before The End. I stare a few seconds longer, hoping she'll feel it, but she bawls into her hands, face hidden. Tooth moves his hand into mine. A pulse passes through us.

"*I was going to get everything right . . .*" Rattail sings again. None of us have ever gotten anything right.

Tooth squeezes my hand. I want to kiss him but hold back, stare towards my lap instead. I'm surprised to see my heartbeat vibrating out from below my shirt. I didn't expect it could still work this way.

"*Invert the cross . . . Repossess . . .*" Rattail's words float up from another song, hemorrhaging energy, when Tooth takes me into another room to show me where he sleeps. He sits and pulls me down with him, lights a candle. He leans his back against the wall and I slump against him, my head on his chest. I can smell him: sweat and cigarettes and copper. He offers a dirty hand to me to hold. I bring it to my face: heartline, strong; lifeline, broken; mount, marked by the Star of Solomon.

The ceilings here are slanted, wooden beams covered in magic marker. Band names and logos and phone numbers and poetry are drawn on every inch, just like the plaque outside.

I tell Tooth, "I wish I could write something on the walls," but we don't have anything to write with so he says, "Tell it to me and I'll keep it for you."

I tell him about my deficiencies. I tell him about dreams that follow me around. I tell him about the smell of the ocean. I tell him about my indecencies and heavy scarring, about the persistent confessions between the heel of my hand and my inner elbow.

Tooth says, "There must have been times you were happy," and I was.

"Like when?" he asks.

Like the day me and Aimee existed in the lush expanse between cigarette drags and swigs of luxury. When we first became friends one of the earliest favours she did for me was bring me back into morning light. Before Aimee I looked like I'd just climbed out of a warm pool on a cool day.

One of my favourite things was Aimee's kitchen table, wooden and warm under our elbows. One morning we sat there with a jar of cherries between us, spooning candied red into tall skinny glasses of Coca-Cola. The drinks would bubble as the cherries sunk to the bottom. We'd sip, swirl our straws, dip our fingers in to get to the syrup-soaked fruit.

Carbonation nibbled at Aimee's thumb and forefinger, blind eyes to bait. She pulled out the cherries one by one, sucking them clean of cola. A plastic sword in my wallet, a lime green cocktail souvenir from a night I barely remembered, speared a row of cherries in my own glass, and I popped them off their skewer one by one.

After breakfast we went to Value Village and found jeans that suctioned onto the thin fat of our butts, fitting so well no one noticed when we walked out wearing them.

At the park we twisted our swings to see who could spin the fastest. Aimee's chain wrapped so tight a link snapped. Her arm disappeared in the sand, her cheek dipped in for a dusting. She came up spitting brown granules from her mouth before she could laugh. The broken link had landed a foot away. I shoved it into my pocket, later added it to my collection of charms.

We're laying down now and Tooth is pulling me close, arms around my chest. "I'm going to fall asleep like this," I tell him and he says, "so am I."

Me and Hunter always slept touching, his knees behind mine, face in my hair. I'd wake up sometimes with my head buried in his neck, or drooling on his chest.

I wake up and for a second forget where I am, who I'm with. I wake up and think we're here, me and Hunter, together, that we've been asleep this whole time. But Tooth has a different way of breathing, a different amount of pressure in his muscles, and my senses catch up to these discrepancies.

I expect to be disappointed, but I'm surprised instead by relief. To be here, in these arms. A small streak of guilt tries to work its way through me but I don't let it in, don't let myself think too long about confusing Tooth for Hunter.

There's a scratching in the walls, must be what woke me up. Tooth must be used to the sound because his breathing is steady, solid. I count his breaths and let them draw me back to sleep.

I dream of eating metal spoons. They melt halfway to my mouth. What I manage to get in dribbles hot metal down my chin. I pull layers of skin from my face trying to pick it off.

I dream of heavy boots laced tight along my arms. I walk on all fours, knees unprotected, feet bare. Crawl through roads until I am on my childhood street. Crawl to my old house but when I get there it's turned into the Mission. Jupiter's fallen so far out of the sky that it's only a foot away from the club's roof. I hold the planet's knowledge and know it hasn't fallen as far as it needs to yet, but if anyone steps into the Mission I wouldn't be able to tell them how much more time they'd have before the planet crunches through the roof. I'm sworn to secrecy and will lose all powers if I say a thing. I go into the club anyway because I have no choice. It's how my story has to end.

I dream I am dressed in teeth, shoulders hard and on the defense. Aimee appears beside me. She bounces on the balls of her feet and so I do the same: speed buzz. The muscles of our calves are caught in the crosshairs of our fishnets. We both bounce as we wait for a red light to change to green because green means go.

We go.

I wake up and wonder: Where did Aimee and Tara go? I can't remember the last time I saw them at the party. I can't remember if we said goodbye.

The whiskey and grayline have left a hangover that reaches all the way to my eyebrows. There's a chemical sting in my sinuses, peroxide expulsions.

I slide away from Tooth, careful not to wake him. I sit up and find the house fits me like eyes from across the room, teasing each hair up off my arms.

The mirror in the hallway is cracked, only half of it still nailed to the wall. A black spatter runs through my reflection, falls in freckles across my cheeks. Halfway down the staircase I can hear two guys talking, going over their route to get to Montreal. I feel shy, don't want to be seen coming down without Tooth even though I know no one would care.

There are other bedrooms but no one's in them. It's hard to tell if they've already been packed up and cleared out of anything valuable. There are a few clothes, paperback books. It could be trash. It could be everything.

There's a small hole in the wall of a near empty bedroom. I crouch beside it, hoping for a sign of who was here before Shit Kitten. I feel around for a bobby pin, or a letter tucked away. Something rolls under my finger—a sow bug tucked into a ball maybe. I leave it where it is, wipe the dust on my leg and go back to Tooth. He's awake when I come in, but still in bed. His arm comes up, invites me back in.

"I'm leaving today," he says.

"I know."

We go out the back door. Tooth cups his hands into a bucket of rainwater and tells me to drink. When the water's gone I kiss his palm.

He drinks after me. We kiss with renewed mouths. "Where's your charm bracelet?" he asks.

I hold up my wrist and show him the bare silver links. "I lost all the charms a long time ago."

He slides an earring out of his left ear. It's an eye. Blue, the same colour as his. "Someone gave this to me once," he says. "For protection from bad luck."

"I'll lose it, just like the other ones," I tell him. "These things don't work for me anymore."

"Wear it," he says. "I want you to have it."

I get on my bike. Aimee's and Tara's are gone. They must be at home.

"You don't have to stay here, you know," Tooth says. "You could come with me."

I could.

"I can't," I tell him. "Not without Aimee, at least."

"Why don't you both leave?"

I don't have an answer for this as I ride away. My head pounds in time with the push of my bike pedals and I need to stop every ten feet. On the front of a lawn sits a birdbath, its base thick with algae. I drink from it anyway, desperate.

Back at the house Tara's on the front steps. I almost don't recognize her at first with her wig off and her black hair flattened to her scalp and stinking with sweat trapped for days under acrylic and nylon. She doesn't look up as I come towards the porch. Her face is ten years older and straight with pain, lit cigarette held to her arm.

"What are you doing?" I ask.

She doesn't answer immediately, just keeps her head down as the skin blisters up.

"Watch," she says, moving to another burn on her arm, something that's a little less fresh than what she just made. She pulls a safety pin from her pocket and leaks the blister before carefully tearing open the flap of skin. She doesn't pull it all the way off, just makes an opening. She breaks open a cap of grayline and sprinkles it on, pulls the skin flap back down and rubs the powder into the blister.

"This is the best way to get a buzz," she says. "Hits you way faster through a wound than through the stomach."

Soon her arms will crawl with cuts and burns, bruises the size of quarters. In a dream I had a long time ago my skin turned into fossils pocked with the spirit shells of millipedes and crayfish. The fossils were soft to the touch and full of water, like sponges.

This is what I'm seeing in Tara right now as her eyes roll, her hands wander. She makes a vague motion for me to sit beside her. I come down to her level and she leans over, her face against mine. She licks my cheek and leaves a slow trail of shine leading to the corner of my lip.

Tara passes out on the porch minutes later. I pull her up, drag her in with me. Leaving her outside would mean leaving her for the dogs.

Cam is skinning an animal in the kitchen. The smell is more fecal than anything. He's mumbling the lyrics to a Shit Kitten song like the stink doesn't faze him. I recognize the tune to "PostApoc." I have to cover my nose and mouth just to get past him.

"Aimee's still asleep," he says.

Aimee never sleeps this long. "Is she sick?" I want to know, but Cam's already moved his attention back to the blood and bone on the kitchen floor.

Aimee's asleep in the same clothes she had on the night before. She doesn't move when I come into the room. I lie down beside her and shake her, gently.

She jumps awake. "How long have I been asleep for?" she asks.

"Not sure," I tell her. "You okay?"

"I'm just really, really tired," she says. "You okay?"

"Yeah, I stayed with Tooth."

"They're probably on their way out of the city by now, huh?"

I brush something wet from my eye.

"Probably," I say.

22

LIMP BESIDE ME

Aimee threw up this morning and has been sleeping ever since so me and Tara are on our own to pick up today.

My body's too rundown for this. I don't even want a drink and barely even want to smoke, but Tara's desperate and I can't let her go alone now, not after what happened to Aimee. Tara wanted to go to Chris's place because it's the closest option.

"What if they rape us, too?" I ask, reminding Tara of what Aimee told us later about what happened there: the force of strong hands over her abdomen, warm breath moving in at her ears, the smell of male whiskers that lingered on her face for days afterwards.

"Mike's isn't really that far," I tell her. I feel like I have as much energy as Aimee does these days and don't want to be doing this at all, but Tara gives in to me and so does relief.

We push forward. Within three blocks of Mike's house we get circled anyway. Four men eye us, grab our handlebars. Tara goes limp beside me, ready to offer up the peaks of her hips.

Say something. Say anything, I tell myself. But the men only sniff and then back away in a blur of basic vocabulary. We are too thin, dried wafers with nothing for them, not even the energy to lift our heads, let alone theirs.

My adrenaline doesn't even kick in. My body must really be shutting down. I wonder if Mike has any food. I will cuddle with him just for that.

We pull up to Mike's as a girl climbs out of the dark dead bushes in his front yard. She's the only other person I've ever seen coming out of here, but I wonder if she was visiting with Mike, or just sleeping outside.

This girl's got a black eye and is wearing only one shoe. No makeup of course. Her legs are a patchwork of sores and her balance sputters. She flails, disrupts the air with every uneven step.

A second girl climbs out behind her. She leaves a scent of sticky fingerprints, private sheddings, genital mishaps. I blush as water rushes through my mouth.

The girls walk by as if they don't even see us. Maybe we're not really here. The sun's been stuck on sunset all day, but we're sweating. I've wrapped a black bandana around my breasts for a top. Tara's t-shirt is cropped by a knot at the waist.

Mike sizes up our bare stomachs when he sees us at the door. I look for a leer in his eyes but they shift too quickly as Tara practically pushes him into the bedroom. I wonder if she'll even bother waiting for me after she gets what she wants.

When it's my turn, I ask Mike if he can feed me and he says he's got dried kidney beans and a bit of brown rice but that he needs to eat, too, so we'll have to split something. We count the beans. We'll get ten each.

He doesn't ask me to tell him anything but I do anyway, about how I forgot about food when I was out in Vancouver. We all did. When we did eat, though, it was packaged cakes, a lot like the ones Cam and Trevor found a while back. We'd smoke half a cigarette, stub it out, and bite into something vanilla with white icing in the middle.

I'd watch as Hunter would stab an index finger—dirty nail and skin nicotine yellow—into the soft melt of sugar to bring a drop of icing taste to my tongue. One poke at a time, until the two halves of the cake were clean. Then we'd smoke the other half of the cigarette we'd stubbed out and, with shiny fingers, pick at the golden yellow sponge between drags, neither of us ever eating a whole cake by ourselves.

By Christmas of that year we were all twelve pounds lighter and had black-on-black vision, eyeliner thick to keep details relegated to the interconnectedness of depth and death perception. I can't remember what the rest of the band and their girlfriends did, but me and Hunter spent Christmas Day at a rep cinema, paid two dollars each to see *The Man Who Fell to Earth*. My bottom lip trembled until the last credit rolled but my eyes never spilled over. Dehydrated. Just like now.

We didn't know where else to go after the movie because everything was closed, so we stayed in our seats. Hunter presented me with a gift of oil paints, a small palette of violence and despair. Together we read the names of each hue slowly:

Gash

Bruise

Solitude

Corpse

We were killing time until we killed ourselves.

Mike's kitchen table is plastic, not the welcoming wood of Aimee's old table but good enough. As I expected, Tara is already gone when I come out of the bedroom.

"More food for us then," Mike says as I look out the front window for her.

Mike wants to eat together. I'm so hungry that I will say yes to anything. He builds a fire in the backyard to boil water for the rice. "It'll take a while," he says.

"I don't care. That's fine."

I eat my food in two bites. Mike talks, says everyone he knew is gone now, no friends left.

"Maybe you could be my friend," he says.

"Maybe," I shrug. I have to remind myself to add a smile.

My body doesn't have the energy to digest everything, so I ask Mike if I can sleep here. He wants to sleep beside me. I let him.

It's dark out when I wake up. The sun has finally gone down but there's no way to measure what time it might actually be. Beside me, Mike is talking in his sleep, repeating, "I can't do this anymore. I can't do this anymore. I can't do this anymore."

I can't do this anymore, either.

I slip away, out of the bedroom, out of the house, and I ride. The beginning of a new cold is scratching at the back of my throat when I get back to the Victorian to find Tara in the closet again, hoarding her own trip.

Aimee's rubbing a bloated belly. I ask her how she's feeling and she says there must have been something off with the meat

Cam and Trevor caught the other day. "Now I know how you feel," she says.

In another eight hours my sinuses will be clogged. I lie down and imagine a fever tingling along the back of my neck. I know it's more in my head than anything but I can't stop making myself sweat.

Aimee closes the door on Tara so we can have some privacy. She slides down beside me and says, "Remember what it was like to be thirteen? I had a fantasy then. Maybe my first fantasy. About boys. No one in particular, just in general. I liked to think about them as skinny with long hair, chains coming out of their back pockets. I liked to think of them as depressed or damaged, as people I could save. The boys in my mind always smoked and always drank and always listened to music when they were alone and thinking too much, too hard.

"I liked to fantasize that they would gravitate to me. Need me above anyone else, that somehow they would know I could instantly understand them.

"I used to look for these boys outside convenience stores or in parking lots, or standing in line to get into a show. I would hope we could spend the whole day together. I'd let them put their heads in my lap and I would just stroke their hair and listen to everything they had to tell me."

"Did you ever kiss in your fantasies?" I ask.

"Not usually, no. We would just hug, hold each other, be platonic soulmates, instantly connected."

"Like you and me."

"Yeah, Ang. Just like you and me."

Aimee falls asleep and leaves me thinking about how it felt to be thirteen. It's a memory that tastes like doughnuts and premium cigarettes. It's something the colour of cherry red hair dye and a blue spring sky.

I touch Aimee's hair and she whimpers. I swallow and my throat fights it.

23

SURVIVAL GUIDE

Aimee throws up again the next morning. She hangs her head out the bedroom window and lets it go.

I rub her stomach to help calm it down. The flesh is hard and I worry about something I heard once, that internal bleeding makes your stomach firm up. I don't say this out loud.

I worry about parasites and tumours, dysentery and Crohn's disease. I don't say this out loud, either. I don't say much at all because I've woken up with the raw throat I knew I'd have. The air in the room is hot, immovable. Aimee is too dizzy to talk. I want to ask if she's been able to eat at all since this started but I'll wait for her nausea to pass first.

Aimee falls asleep. I catch a swathe of Tara's back as she slinks out of the room and down the stairs. The door falls closed behind her a minute later. I assume she's off to pick up. I wait a beat, and then I go, too, but not after Tara.

It's a crash worship at the lake: the water has returned and the tide has finally come in. Needy, it soaks through my boots, makes a successful attempt at getting under my clothes. It laps and laps at my legs, my arms, and I lie down and let it wash over me.

The waves will soon be reaching for Shelley and Anadin's cabin if the tide comes in any closer. It might want them more than I do.

Today, everything around here stares. Anadin says the devil bore its rites through visualization and has been realized here. She sits crosslegged on the floor with Shelley. Their ears have turned feline, twitch with periscope hearing. On the wall behind them, a mounted wolf's head gnashes its glazed teeth. Shelley says it won't threaten me unless I face it head on.

A tease, all of this. They invite me to sit and spread seven cards between us. Shelley reads the first. "Ten of hearts. Would've been a good omen of a long and happy life if it wasn't upside down."

I want to tell them about the tide, that it's getting closer, but my voice won't come out.

Anadin reads. "Queen of clubs. Signifying the number forty. Another symbol of cheer. Does this mean we'll have wine soon?" she asks, looking to Shelley.

I want to tell them I could probably help them find wine, but I don't say anything. They must know the same channels we've all been using. What else is there? Shelley just keeps reading.

"Jack of clubs. Disorder and failure. A failed venture."

I want to tell them that card is all my fault, my responsibility, but I don't say anything.

Anadin reads. "Ten of clubs. A tower surrounded by clouds. Denotes sickness, maybe death."

I want to tell them to stop reading the cards, but I don't say anything.

Shelley reads. "Another from the suit of clubs. A lot of dark strength today. False friends, or faltering friends, maybe. In better times, though, this could indicate a new love."

I want to tell them there are other things present here, but I don't say anything.

Anadin reads. "The seven of hearts. A change in residence. Does it look like that's something that will happen sooner or later?"

I want to tell them it could happen for them today if the water gets in here, but I don't say anything.

Shelley reads. "The six of hearts. I wish it was the three of hearts instead. This one is so dependent on present conditions. Everything is too weak right now for this to prosper."

I want them to tell me why I'm here because I can't remember the reason I came. Instead, Shelley says, "We saw a horned god, Ang. Do you know what that means?"

"It could have been a horned *dog*, Shelley," Anadin says.

"I know what I saw."

Outside, a wave crashes against the side of the cabin. Water speckles the window. Shelley and Anadin act like they don't notice, just keep talking.

Anadin: Just in case, we created a circle in the sand. To invoke the planetary spirits.

Shelley: We needed virgin parchment to write on but we didn't have any, so we clipped some skin from the stuffed animals on the walls.

Anadin: We couldn't get anything from the birds.

Shelley: We asked for abyss.

Anadin: We asked for brothers.

Shelley: We asked for peaceable possession.

Anadin: We asked for fire.

Shelley: We asked for something animal.

Anadin: We asked for divination.

Shelley: We asked for the entitlement to vanitas.

"What did you get?" I ask.

"What do you want?" is their answer. I need an incantation but all they give me is a survival guide, spells they confused for something more.

Another wave hits the cabin. Water's starting to come in under the door. "How much longer do you think this place will stand?" I ask.

"Oh, not long at all," Anadin says.

"You should get going," Shelley adds.

Neither of them move.

"I can help you get some stuff together," I say.

"Oh no," Anadin says. "We're staying here."

"We can't leave our power circle now," Shelley says.

"The one you've drawn in the sand?" I ask. "But it's washed away. The waves—"

"Oh no," Shelley says. "Once it's drawn, it's there forever, even if you can't see it."

"And as long as we remember where we placed it, it will never be broken."

The water's at the cabin again and this time it takes out a window. Shelley and Anadin remain still, their eyes on me.

"Go, Ang," Anadin says.

My clothes dry as I ride back through the city. The sun is out and my stomach is still full of the water I gulped down at the beach when I fell through the waves on the way back to my bike. I ride by an old tavern on Queen Street and brake at the fire escape.

I get to the top of the roof in time to see an office building crumble in the distance. It falls straight down, like an accordian, and disappears in dust. The foundations of the city must be sprouting cracks. A second building goes down minutes later. Its blocks and metal casings fall with such weight that the shake is felt through the streets, all the way up to where I'm sitting.

The world shakes loose in the sky. Mars uproots, falls out of place, drops down beside the moon, which is rising low in the twilight. The city's foundations aren't just cracking; all foundations are. I think about Tooth and wonder what the view is like in Montreal. I spent so many nights believing in apocalyptic mindsets but never thought about the hunger. Never understood what this pain would be like, that it would be endless, insatiable.

The lake water must have been bad because my stomach's cramping with gas. A burp bubbles up in my chest and it brings with it the taste of whiskey from Tooth's party, which was at least three days ago. It must be rotting in the lining of my stomach.

In all our talk about The End, before it really happened, I never expected to feel so haunted, either. At least no more than what I'd already felt. Hunter used to tell me that everything is haunted.

"It's just ruined beauty," he said. "Spirits get into people, possess them, and their beauty starts to decay. Ghosts feed on your youth. We're all potential sacrifices. The more powerful the spirit is that chooses you, the more damaged you become."

"But that's good, right?"

"Of course," he said. "Everyone wants to be chosen."

"When did you start seeing ghosts?" I asked.

"When I was young I started seeing them here and there, but the day after I met you, I started seeing them all over the place."

I remember a lyric he wrote for a song he never finished: *"The devil dug . . . the devil dug . . ."*

The earth shakes again but I don't want to come down off the roof. A couple of raccoons have been sniffing around my bike. I'll wait for them to move on now before I can go anywhere. At least the sun isn't at its highest point. I pull out the survival guide Anadin and Shelley gave me.

"EVERYTHING HATH HIS OWN NATURAL VIRTUES, BY WHICH EVERYTHING IS A BEGINNING OF A MARVELOUS EFFECT."

—THE BOOKE OF SECRETES

The psychology of survival goes like this: it's a time-dishonoured technique, a diagram of a wilderness whose texture I can't bear. Together we could build a passive outlook into the areas where the forbidden path is the most difficult to master. It requires the skill of a firestarter and the cunning of a left-hand belief.

Survival medicine suggests to find a yellow-flowered plant, a handful of leaves, a pint of water to purify the blood. Mix it with wine to sleep soundly. Amethyst improves the memory. The memory improves the experience. (On the side of the road, you will find neither.)

For food: put a pebble in the mouth to suppress the appetite.

The body's loss of water tempered with the memory of a sanitary surface: tile and antisepctic, soap and water, enema and edibility. It must have been a mistake because I am just waiting.

Skin flakes. Dehydrate. Develop a rash as the most obvious and effective way to communicate.

Taste buds demystified by the knowledge and skills it takes to build shelter before being consumed by a starving anchor. What does this city's surface hide in its connected fatigue? Exhaustion holds more in its bowels than the loose teeth of an average organism.

Commit to memory: what you can stomach, the arena of your ecosystem. The sounds of a certain voice, any voice will do, to counteract loneliness. Rational or irrational, it's your choice. Choose your friends wisely.

There will be light unbelievable, rumbling and sliding through prolonged exposure.

Without the aid of standard navigational devices you will have to rely on the passage of an omen. Even with survival training people die. They don't know that building a fire is what keeps spirits under control, not what summons them. Mentality and interconnectedness are key: no training required when you recognize panic as sustenance.

The will to survive is exaggerated. The closer to death you've been the clearer your priorities. It's an acquired skill that strings together the knowledge of dark sunken eyes and skin's elasticity due to stress.

Sleep with a wolf's head and it will bring sound dreams. Carry a piece of its meat in your pocket to heat your whole body.

Survival stresses can produce flashbacks. If poorly transmitted, these visions will rely on hindsight and healthy retinas to be experienced. You must accept them because they will prepare you for the toughest times.

Your personal hygiene standards impact the rolling of your intestines. Are your teeth loose enough yet? Even sweat and urine can pull them out. Strands of sputum like nylon thread.

Stay clean without luxury. Special attention is needed to the feet, underarms, crotch, hands and hair, all the prime areas for infestation. Infection of the erotic. When water is scarce take an air bath. The removal of the clothes will bring a sacrifice to the sun. The heat will burn away mites and odours.

Soap can be made from animal fat and wood ashes. Sigils on soiled paper make the most powerful talismans. If you want to save time and combine this to become a primary ritual, rub a thumbnail of fat over your pubic bone and allow your body to act as a makeshift altar.

To simply make soap, extract the grease from the fat of an animal. Boil it and stir frequently until the fat is rendered. If you don't have enough water make your own by teasing your gag reflex. Don't bring yourself to the point of vomiting, only to the point of excessive salivation.

What requires divination: when emotional needs take precedence over the physical. A blood relic can change this but can't be obtained from the slabs of ice-blue bodies blocking the subway tunnels. Never draw blood without performing the proper rituals. In the 1970s witches substituted wine for blood for the diabolic proportions of their inverted pentacles. Consecrated, the earth you will sleep on will decrease susceptibility to severe shock. Consider the results of bodily loss: a tingling sensation in the phantom limbs, dim vision, swollen tongue, an echo in the chamber of the heart, numbness, painful urination.

Ill-applied survival tactics can result in symptoms similar to every day of your life: something too close to a bad hangover to recognize as anything different. Symptoms are a first-cousin to depression and may result in death if left untreated.

Atmospheric temperatures account for a daily exertion that must be replaced with a palm sacrificed to chiromancy. Celsius and Fahrenheit have graduated to constellations, gods in the sky creating intense activity, lower altitudes, low-degree burns in the esophagus. You must replace the water they make you lose.

Emotional instability and low urine output, delayed capillary refill and a trench line down the center of the tongue: it could be a bad dream and a slow waking on a Saturday morning or it could be the rest of your life's daily routine. The parallels are defeating.

Rival your acclimatization. The body performs inefficiently when you conserve sweat but not water. Limit extreme conditions. Practice thought control. Ration your daily intake of panic and anxiety. Lick the salt off your armpit to boost sodium and electrolytes. A t-shirt soaked with sweat can hold as much as three-quarters of a litre of fluids. Your body is a self-sustaining cycle of loss and life. Drink up.

You've kept your finger on your pulse your whole life and been disappointed every time. Although you can live several weeks without food you need an adequate amount under severe discretions. Lack of willpower means better retention of essential vitamins, minerals and salts. An inadequate caloric intake could lead to cannibalism in the wild but the only wilderness to contend with is the exotic hallucination of a bare ocean and an imbalance of bird bone and hard, canine surfaces.

Strike the earth. Properly exorcise any stones used in multiple rituals. Estimate fluid loss by measuring heart and breathing rates.

A wrist pulse rate at a hundred beats per minute means a breathing rate of twelve to twenty breaths per minute and should be approached with affection. This is not yet death, only lucid dreaming.

A wrist pulse rate at a hundred to a hundred and twenty beats per minute means a breathing rate of twenty to thirty breaths per minute and should be approached with care. This is not yet death, only a tool and technique to tap into the spirit world.

A wrist pulse rate at a hundred and twenty to a hundred and forty beats per minute and thirty to forty breaths per minute indicates vital signs should be approached with awe. This is the moment we've all been waiting for.

For now, breathe. The pop of life under your skin has tenacity.

Dogs have pushed the raccoons out and are now circling below. I consider jumping from this roof to the next but don't trust my spatial judgment, or the strength of my legs. It looks like it's only two, maybe three feet, but I can see myself missing by a step, hands clawing down the brown brick.

Something round and hard bounces off my head. From the sky, a clattering of brown hail. I get hit again, step back, and something crunches under me. It's not hail falling from the sky, but snails. The sky must be eating its own tail and is squeezing out whatever's getting sucked up in its coils.

I crouch under a hooded air vent, snails crunching under me with every step. The clouds above turn an oily grey, a colour I've never seen come over them before.

I don't know how long I've been awake today but fatigue is coming on. My thoughts are spinning out and I'm mumbling, "Our skulls will be replicated in a painting on a telephone pole. If the collapse of everything isn't coming right at this moment, then it will be any day now. We just have to be ready, find a way to focus on—what? A belief you would like to touch. A reach that gets beyond a spiritual void, even though that gap is the size of a cavern.

"Find a way to focus on an extra coating, a haze poised to be devoured."

If I could wish for anything right now it would be for this to stop. So I can get off this roof and back to Aimee.

I might have just wished the last wish on earth because the clattering breaks off. Around me are thousands of snails. I stretch out my strides to kill as few as possible but the crunch under my weight is still disquieting, leaving an oozing trail.

The raccoons aren't circling anymore. They must have taken cover from the falling shells. I clear the ladder two rungs at a time and get on my bike, head back to the house.

24

BEFORE EVERYTHING BREAKS APART

Something's crawled into the Victorian. Cam's blaming Tara, says she brought it home with her while he was out with Taser, but Tara says it found its way through the front door on its own.

It's in the living room now, making the continuous sound of a small world folding in on itself. Its body consists of two girls in one, arms and legs the impossible thinness of a praying mantis. Identical in their plain faces and stringy hair, their sunken eyes, they stare at us from violet irises but remain mute. Instead of mouths they have slashes. Their double body fits into one chair, limbs a puzzle of sticks clasping in place.

We all stand in the living room doorway, watching, afraid to move, afraid to turn our backs. Tara's the only one not with us.

"She's upstairs," Aimee says. "Doing what, I don't know."

Not even Taser, who snaps at everyone but Cam, will come into the house. "So much for a guard dog," Aimee says, earning a "fuck you" from Cam.

Below us, a leaden scrape across the basement floor. A dead man's incoherent shouts follow a few seconds later. Even the spirits are disturbed by what's in here now.

Upstairs, Tara's found an old tube of lipstick under a mattress and tried it on. She wipes her mouth with the back of her hand and crimson red smears down the side of her face. She looks at me and says, "Where'd you get to for so long?" The question comes through the lipstick slit, as if she's just made a new mouth in her cheek.

I don't answer, just stare back her, speechless in the reflection of her eyes' infected abyss.

Cam and Trevor move their stuff into our bedroom. We lock the door behind us to keep out whatever's still in the living room downstairs.

It's so hot that everyone takes off their shirts. The window's wide open and the air's got the same humid electricity as a summer storm, but it's swamp-still. Not even a breeze is getting in.

Energy ripples through the heat of the room. Cam offers up some grayline. I don't really want to do any but don't know what else to do to get through this.

Energy ripples through the heat of our words. Shamans, each of us. At least we'd like to think when we're high like this.

Now that we're all buzzing, Tara reconnects. Together, we go into a trance, and without her speaking I hear her tell us, "It occupies everything, this addiction. I never thought this would happen, or at least not so fast. I thought if any of us would get hooked it would be Ang, because she's already given herself up and away so much. Every day I think, 'This must be right near the end.'"

Tara is at the door now, fumbling with the lock. It's stuck. "I need out right now," she says.

Cam gets up, jiggles the handle, and Tara's out. We hear her run through the house and out the back door. We watch through the window as she braces herself against the porch railing. Taser bucks against his chain, barking wildly in Tara's direction.

A few weeks ago Tara thought she would never need a washroom again. Some people's bodies are either adapting or shutting down, everything turning to gristle inside. Now Tara's innards are turning to liquid, language projectile.

Aimee tells me to go help her and I get there in time to watch Tara choke in reverse on a ball of blue hair, same as her wig. She spits up a four-leaf clover, a crucifix, a cat with green gemstone eyes.

Her body, previously filled with black and bile and bone, has started to rebuild from the ash of grayline. The dead are coming to reclaim their bodies and are siphoning from Tara's, bleeding her nutrients, her bone density, her remaining muscle mass.

Tara spits out red laces that could fit a pair Doc Marten boots. The backs of her hands shed white-blonde hair, opposite to what grows from her head. In documented cases of possession, it's been noted that the possessed vomit objects: hair clips and bones and eyes. If grayline's ingredients include the ashes of the dead, are we voluntarily possessing their spirits?

Tara says she's just hallucinating. "It's like I'm having a vision of thinning blue jeans and an empty market stall and a flare of fraying denim over the tops of Converse high tops. The laces are undone and the feet inside are bare. The person has a face but all I can see is a thick patch of pubic hair growing from the cream of pale cheeks, flecks of dirt matted into coarse brown clumps."

Tara's words cut off just in time for her to heave out sagging cargo pockets of bad directions. Her tongue's as dry as a cat's.

"This might be right near the end, before everything breaks apart," she says out loud this time.

Tara's body is uncontrollable, head rocking back with a dusting of laughter that starts out as a gag. Her bladder releases a gentle slide of dirt—cemetery earth. Tara recognizes the smell.

A dog barks. I can't tell if it's from Taser or from Tara. She coughs and it sounds like snapping white teeth clattering across the porch boards. Out comes more gravel and dust, followed by dark, shining things that live under rocks.

The tag on the back of Tara's t-shirt itches in a place she can't reach. I try to help but can't find the right spot. Her shoulder blades are like discs of wax, her hair a wick waiting to be lit on fire.

Tara grabs her middle as if hit with cramps. She squats and her colon sprays twigs. They fly off the porch and make spirals in the dirt, disrupt something black, a squirming body. The bug dislodges, runs disoriented towards Tara's calf. She tries to flick it away but misses. It burrows into the thickest part of her leg.

"This must be right near the end, before everything breaks apart," Tara says again.

She moans and out comes rigor mortis and latent misgivings. A canopy of curls, disappearances, x-ray vision, blue eyeshadow. Closed eyes and quick jabs and something that goes harder, faster, harder, faster.

"This must be right near the end, before everything breaks apart," she says once more.

It's my body and I'll die if I want to.

25

OBITUARY

We don't last long all locked in the same room together. Cam finds half a mickey we'd hid under a pillow and drinks it in three gulps. Ten minutes later he's all over Aimee, kneading her breasts.

"They look bigger than yesterday," he says. "Did they grow overnight?"

Aimee pushes his hand away and moves over, wincing. She looks at me and says, "They're so sore today. I must be getting my period soon. I haven't had it in a while."

Now that Cam's got a taste of alcohol in him he wants more. "Who's coming with me?"

"I'm going to sleep," Aimee says, tired again. Tired all the time these days.

Tara's lying down already, too, an arm draped over her eyes. She doesn't answer.

"I'll go," Trevor says.

"I'll go too," I say.

Downstairs I hear the clink of bicycle chains and the click of Taser's nails on the driveway. The two heads in the living room glare as I move towards the door, looking at me like I've got the taste of something they've always wanted. I finger the earring Tooth gave me.

Later, Aimee finds me on the porch.

"What's going on?" she asks.

"I just can't be inside right now," I say. None of Cam's dealers were around when we'd gone out and the boys weren't ready to give up when I was.

Aimee's skin has turned the colour of ash. She says the girls with the praying mantis body crawled into the basement when she came downstairs. Aimee ran and locked the door behind them. Minutes afterward, the phantom shouts started rising up and haven't stopped. Something's banging on the door, begging to be let out, and we don't know if it's the girls or the ghost.

"A girl who's kept herself close to death long enough that it's left a smell—not of decay but of lilacs and roses just before they turn." That's what I'd want someone to write in my obituary, if there were such things anymore.

I still have the first thing Hunter ever gave me, the only other thing of his I still have: a pressed flower in a compact mirror. I cup it in my hands now, afraid it will disintegrate if it falls out of my orbit. I call this unfortunate. A waste, my life.

When I first see Cam and Trevor running up to the house, it looks like they've caught an animal the way Trevor's cradling warm, red flesh. Taser isn't with them as they bang past us and fly through the front door.

But there's no fresh kill. Trevor's been bitten by Taser. Cam's got him on the living room with a dirty t-shirt wrapped around his hand. Cam is yelling, "Don't just stand there. Fucking HELP US." Having drained the last of our booze earlier, he's washing Trevor's hand with rainwater.

I run upstairs for one of Aimee's pads and a bandana. One of Taser's teeth found a gap between the bones in Trevor's hand and went right through from bottom to top. Fate line severed.

Cam says everyone he knows is out of alcohol. It's the only thing we might be able to use to clean Trevor's hand and hasn't heard of anyone who's still got any. But Cam won't do the same things we'll do for booze, doesn't use the same dealers, even though he's aware of the options.

"I know someone," I say.

Mike tells me he's been dreaming about women's underwear: light pink, lavender, charcoal cotton. He tells me he must be drying out inside because the other day he caught his wrist on a piece of glass but no blood came out. He pulls out a bottle of vodka and tells me, "This is the last one I can give you."

We're sitting at the back of the house. The sun's setting. It's pretty but we don't say so. It's easier not to talk about these things. It's too lonely, and too close to grieving.

Instead Cam says, "Wanna see what I've got?" He reaches into his army pants. There's a crinkling. He pulls out three granola bars. "Expired, but whatever," he says. "They'll still be good."

My stomach growls. I hadn't noticed I was hungry. Cam offers me one. Chocolate chip and marshallow. My teeth ache over the honeyed oats. Cam sees my eye on the leftover bar.

"Wanna split it?" he says.

26

CREEP MANIFESTO

Tara walks out of the house with her wig back on and returns wrapped in a blue boa and silver spandex shorts, reciting a creep manifesto like nothing's unusual:

Decree the fate/unwilling
Planetary intercourse/our command is
Far reaching/
For the unchangeable/
Know your fires/
Your cities/
Escape plan C/section off
Earth's ancestors/text collaboration
Creep chronicles/
An un-history

"Hey," she says, giving me full-on eye contact, pupils contracted into speed-sucking focus. Her hands fly through her crooked hair. She's high again but only has another hour left of this buzz. I can tell by the shake in her knee.

"It's a bad taste that can't be killed," she says. "Just like the first time I was ever asked by someone if he could lick the scars inside my arms. When I said yes he flattened his tongue wide across my wrist and worked it all the way up to my elbow. He said there was a taste to it. 'Acquired' was the word he used."

Tara has sacrificed herself as a host to a shadow drug, floored by slim collections of collective delusions. Her posture is a curve that ends in a point: a question mark.

She laughs—split second—and then blanks out before being caught in forward momentum, with it again but not with us.

"I've gotta go, Ang," she says. "I met someone. Someone who knows where to get more grayline. More of everything. They've invited me to stay with them."

"Stay where?" I ask.

"I told him about you," she says, "but he doesn't want a lot of people coming around."

"Where are you going?"

She doesn't answer.

"There's nothing left out there," Cam says.

"That's what they want you to think," Tara says. She leaves everything behind but what she can carry in her purse.

For every hour that Aimee sleeps, which has been most of them lately, Trevor's hand blackens by another inch, no matter how much vodka we pour onto it. The infection's spreading fever directly to his brain.

"ANG," he says. "I've figured out EVERYTHING." I wait for him to tell me what everything is but instead a sob comes out of him.

It feels like it might be what we used to know as midnight when Cam says, "He's going to have to lose that hand." It might be for another hour that he stares at me as if waiting for permission.

"What do you want me to say?" I ask finally.

"Just tell me what to do."

"I feel like you already know what to do."

It might be two in the morning when Cam looks from one knife to the other. "This one has a sharper blade, but this one can cut deeper."

"Whatever you do, just do it fast," I say.

Trevor's pillow is soaked with sweat but he's shivering through fever.

"I don't want to be here for this," I tell Cam.

Trevor's eyes are closed.

"Fine, then go." Cam doesn't look at me when he says this. He's looking at Trevor.

I only have two cigarettes left. Again. Aimee must have a few; she's hardly been awake enough to smoke any. Not sure what'll be left after this, if anything.

Outside, the night air's got a chill in it. I'm in a t-shirt but don't want to go back inside. It's easier to be cold.

I'm a block away from the house when I hear a short, gruff cry. It could have come from the Victorian, but it also could just be an animal. I can't let myself ponder it any more than that. Instead I think about Hunter: past life and what was wrong and what was right and what really mattered. Did we really matter? Yeah, I think we did.

We spent so much time nurturing boredom and defense that our expressions took on early lines of flawed character. Every question I asked him started with an unraveling and ended the same way, but I was only a catalyst for one of them.

I remember my ear against the mild swell of his pectoral, the rock of bone beneath a dark cavity, an obscurity where the heart should have been. When I get to him, finally, will we be able to work our way back to what we had?

I walk the same four blocks until the sun comes up, consider myself lucky that it even makes an appearance for me today. I didn't want to be back in that house in the dark.

Cam and Trevor are gone when I get there, along with their clothes, books and knives. Trevor's mattress is bare. There is as much blood left behind as I'd expected. It's the blood on Aimee's crotch that surprises me, scares me.

Her face is that of someone drowning, lips blue and slightly swollen.

"I have the worst cramps right now," she says. "I might puke. This is the worst period I've ever had."

The window is open all the way but there's no air coming in. Nothing moves outside. Aimee's hair is plastered to her forehead. I crouch down beside her but she sits up and bolts for the bathroom. The bedroom door slams open against the wall and shakes on its hinges.

On Aimee's bed is a circle of blood—more than the start of a period. I run into the bathroom after her. She's curled up on the floor, red soaking her jean shorts like piss. Her left hand covers her abdomen like she's trying to calm whatever's inside.

I kneel over her, try to get her on her back, but she keeps her body coiled. "Let me," I say, reaching for the button of her shorts. They don't even need to be undone they're so loose, but I give her time by popping the waistband, unzipping the fly before pulling them toward her ankles.

I'm not ready for the smell of so much menstrual blood. In this heat it could rot on her body; its odour already holds a hint of heavy brown.

Aimee's panties are soaked all the way up to the waist. I peel them away and a strand of mucous breaks from between her legs. She's breathing fast now.

"Relax," I say.

"Ang," she says, "it hurts."

"I know. I won't last, though."

Her midsection contracts and another stream of blood pushes out from her. "Shit, Ang," she says. "What's happening?"

I wanted to bring her back to bed but she said she didn't want to move just yet. That might have been three hours ago. We're still on the bathroom floor, my body against her back, arm overtop of hers, leg wrapped over her hip. Together, we shake. Her shivering is violent enough for both of us. I can't let her chill take me over. She needs all the heat I have.

With everyone gone now but us, the house is the quietest it's ever been. There isn't even a skitter from the ghosts upstairs or down. In the night, I tell Aimee, "Breathe."

She breathes.

In a dream I'm cutting the anchor tattoo out of Aimee's arm to keep us weighted down. In another dream I realize I've fallen asleep too long to remind Aimee to breathe. Beside me, she's gone stiff. I am no longer in a dream.

Overnight Aimee's body has gained the volume of death and I've lost all muscle mass. I cover her with the blanket left on Tara's bed because I don't know what else to do.

Miscarriage. From that pick up she did alone.

I am on my own in a way I've never been before, but now, more than any other time in my life, I have the feeling of being closed into a crowd: mental crush of space, claustrophobic estimates, emotional perception in overdrive.

I believe I've made a mistake in waking. I go back to sleep to see if I can correct my reality. But every time I start to fall asleep I think of Aimee's body beside me and get an adrenaline jolt. It would be easier not to think at all.

It's my body and I'll die if I want to.

27

AFTERBIRTH

Aimee's already decomposing, decaying in fast-forward. Her tattoos are shriveled but the colour's still solid. I know I should move her, but I'm not ready. At least with her body still here, I can feel a little less alone.

I don't wear my own clothes anymore. I live in hers. Aimee's sweatshirt fits me like a dress. In it, I soak in my own sweat.

I wait two days before I close the bathroom door but the smell still gets through the hallway. It's dark green with spots of maroon. By now I thought I knew what death smelled like. If I sit with her body long enough and talk to her, I can get used to the scent. The only problem is, it seems like it gets worse by the hour.

I wait two more days after that before moving downstairs because the smell is all over the second floor now. There's a mark on the kitchen ceiling below Aimee's body. Is she leaking through the floor?

I can't sleep here at night because the smell's gotten outside. The animals know what I'm hiding in here and they claw and cry to get in.

Aimee's skin is as green and bloated as the smell that comes off her. I love her too much to let her see how nauseous she makes me, so I gulp it down and suck it up as I cup her skull lightly, so her scalp doesn't come away in my hands. I run my fingers through her hair until strands come loose between my knuckles. I braid the stray hairs and tie them around my wrist.

I don't have much to pack: a lighter with its last bit of flame, a few t-shirts, my black faux-fur jacket.

I finally take off Aimee's hooded sweatshirt. It will be too hot to wear it on my bike. As I stuff it into my bag a single scream comes out of the basement, the same scream as the day we arrived.

Outside, the wind whips tight, a bed sheet snapping flat over the city. A gust cracks something thin and light—a blade of grass maybe—across the bridge of my nose, vicious enough to open a thin red line.

I turn around, look one last time at the house. Just in case Aimee's standing in the window. Just in case it's not really over. But there's nothing left but ghosts.

I take a bike but just walk with it for now. On my way to the beach I unclasp the bare silver charm bracelet and pull on it hard from each end. The links come apart, fall away from each other and into the cracks of the sidewalk. There's no luck left in it. I finger the eye dangling from my ear and hope that the bracelet's failings don't mean there isn't any luck left at all.

Shelley and Anadin's house is gone. The lake has retreated again, too, left the bare bones of their caged birds to bleach in the sun.

"Ang!" The voice comes from a crop of trees a hundred feet away.

Off the beach, Shelley and Anadin look thinner, older, like they left parts of themselves back there with their bird bones. They've set up a small area between the trees, built benches and beds out of piled flat stones.

They had to leave most of their things behind. Shelley holds up a violin. One of its strings is broken and has curled underneath the hem of her dress. She sees me looking at it but doesn't make a move to fix it.

"We've been trying to recreate the earth's atmosphere again," she says. The veins in her neck go varicose when she speaks. Her skull has widened, chin extended. Shelley and Anadin both have exaggerated faces now, complexions blanched and eyes fixed in a start: cats alerted.

"Did you notice anything different today?" Shelley asks.

"I don't think it's working like we thought it would," Anadin says before I can answer, putting her husky-cold eye on me. "Let's go to the beach," she says, swaying her head south for me to follow.

"Do you still dream?" Anadin asks when we hit the stained line where the tide hit hardest.

"I do," I say.

"Then that means we're right about it," she says.

"Right about what?" I ask.

They stop to sit. I come down on my knees and sit on my ankles. The circulation in my legs stops almost immediately.

"About time," Shelley says, pulling a dusty can of tuna out of her bag. Anadin takes a knife from her boot and passes it over.

"You ever heard this theory before?" Anadin says, opening her mouth to let Shelley feed her a bite of tuna. "Well, it's our theory, really, but we believe that you can't be dead if you're still dreaming."

Shelley holds the knife up to me. It's the first time I've seen them with food. Their fast must be broken. The tuna's probably ancient but it still tastes better than anything I've eaten in weeks. "Hang onto that knowledge for when you need it," she says.

"And you will need it," Anadin says.

"You will need this, too," Shelley says, wiping tuna juice from the blade of the knife before handing it to me. "For protection."

"Where are you going to go?" I ask them, folding the knife into my boot.

"We're waiting for the lake to come back for us," Anadin says.

28

MASS(IVE) HALLUCINATION

It feels like I've been riding east for hours already but the sign on the road says I'm still only as far as the old suburbs. I glide into the parking lot of a big mall, its doors long smashed open, department store windows gutted. The sun's coming up and the few bites of tuna I had on the beach with Shelley and Anadin wore off miles back.

The deeper into the mall I get the more light I lose. In the center is a skylight that's also been smashed out. Days' worth of rain has pooled on the floor below. A dead bird has its head tucked against its chest. I get on my knees and cup my hands, take a drink.

Someone's taken the plates of broken glass that would have fallen from the ceiling. The gates of the stores are all drawn down but a lot of them are broken, too. I drift into skeletal clothes racks, find a black cardigan and tie it around my waist. Finally, there's a bulk food store. The bins are down to the crumbs. Mice and rats have replaced what they've taken with their own shit.

"Shit," I say.

"You won't find much around here," says a voice from behind. I spin to face a girl in flared jeans and an army parka, her tangled blonde hair turning to dreads. Look long enough and you can see she used to be pretty.

"You live here?" I ask.

"Yeah," she says, "we do. We live here."

The girl's voice changes then, raises several octaves until it's nearly a child's: "She likes to talk about how we're all in this together but get her alone and see what she'll do for you. She'll write you out of her words and permanently mark you in her own version of the story. This is all going to collapse any day now and if you don't listen to me you'll die this way, eaten alive. Only I'll still be here, under the extra coating of haze and smoke. That's what's been helping me get through this. Will yourself to a paler shade. Command your body."

The girl's eyes roll. Her voice refreshes into something deep and gruff: "This could be like any other night if it weren't for you here right now. There are girls downstairs who'll do anything for ten bucks or a pack of smokes. You want to meet them? You could be one of them if you want."

"Be one of what?" I ask. "What are you?"

But instead of answering me the girl's mouth starts slurring, wordlessly, like it's fallen off its track. Dark liquid drips from under her right sleeve. Her blue eyes go from sky to navy to black and back again.

"Maybe I should just go," I say.

The girl doesn't move. Her legs are in place at a wide stance, her face slack.

I run, through the bulk food store, through its backroom, and out the emergency exit. I don't stop until I'm back on my bike. I ride, and I don't look back this time. My heart doesn't stop pounding until I'm at least twenty minutes away. The adrenaline subsides but the hunger rises again, and with it this time comes weakness, dizziness.

The sun's high and the heat's still bearable but that could change at any minute. I remember Cam and Trevor had looted some houses. Just a few. Why we didn't do it more often I don't know. Maybe we were afraid there'd still be someone inside. Maybe we were afraid of what we'd find. But today I can't afford to be afraid.

I exit off the highway and ride to the border of a residential area. I go for the first house I see: blue vinyl siding, gravel drive-way, porch with peeling white paint, old grey wood exposed underneath.

Everything's intact. I rattle my fingertips across the bay window at the front of the house, wait for movement—nothing. I kick grav-el at the basement windows, wait for movement—nothing. I break a window and slide below ground level. The concrete floor moves. At first I think it's fog but no, it's centipedes, thousands of them, swirling over each other. An inch of a scream squeezes out of me and I clamp a hand over my mouth to keep it shut.

I trip over my shaking legs to get to the stairs, brush bugs from my ankles and calves at the threshold. The ones that hitched a ride up with me scatter off over white carpet and disappear into cracks only they can see.

The upstairs is green upholstery and wooden furniture, a row of stuffed animals on the back of a living room couch. I head to the kitchen and pull the cupboards open, grab at canned meat, cereal, dried peas, crackers, soups. I sniff at half a jar of crunchy peanut butter. A few of the nuts along the top are black but I stuff it in my bag anyway. I'll eat around whatever I have to.

I pull open the drawer and grab kitchen knives and a can opener. Then I go upstairs even though I'm not sure what I'll find up there. Still, I take the stairs two at a time.

My hands blur through costume jewelry and a drawer of old photographs. This house must have belonged to an older woman, or a couple. Grandparents, maybe. I find two hundred dollars stashed under the mattress. I've forgotten what money feels like. I wonder if they still use it where I'm going, decide to take it just in case.

I pull up to a low-rise apartment building, the only structure left standing on a charred block. The curtain's pulled back on a basement window, revealing a smear of blood on the wall and an upturned coffee table. I move on, ride until the sun starts to set.

Off to the left is an old wooden barn, its slats broken off in some places, roof caved in. There's still enough daylight to see that it's empty. I open the canned peas and eat them cold, with my hands. I didn't think to steal a spoon.

I dream of trees split up the middle, rotting from their centers, full of rings of maggots that spill down their trunks. Mushrooms sprout from those same rings: long, yellow-stemmed fungi spreading in skinny bodies down the base of trees, creeping through the grass.

In the dream it's not The End. It's just another day, except for these mushrooms that can pull apart an ancient oak. But that's not all. I walk into a park and it smells of berries and cream, candied soda. A few animals—a couple of dogs or city coyotes, a raccoon—skirt the shade of the tall grass and broken trees.

I have to walk slowly, with my eyes on the park so the dogs don't chase me out. But then I realize they might not even notice; they're smelling the rotten tree rings, licking at residue and slurping maggots and mushrooms. They come away with tongues tinted bright blue from fungal fluids.

No sooner is one stem plucked before another shoots up in its place. No sooner is one stem swallowed than the animal drops, its skull coming apart, cracking open to make room for new growth, the animal's brains used as a house for a new colony of fungi.

DON'T DIE, ONLY DREAM

I wake. Not because of the dream but because of the warmth and wetness at my face: a wolf, white, its snout stinking.

It pulls back when our eyes meet. The sun rises through the slats of the barn, the sky the colour of lavender. The wolf's got the body of a girl: round breasts, narrow waist, tight hips. Hands darker than the rest of her skin.

"Sleep," she says, but her mouth doesn't move.

I dream that the lake has come and gone all over again, dragged Shelley and Anadin in with it. I can't stand its rate of absorption. I can't stand its soft grey surface, a slate magnified to hide what the bowels of this earth have consumed.

On my back in the barn, I spin, land on a memory and a hope. I don't die, only dream:

That you had me by the hair, not hard. Right at the end before we broke apart. Your last grab, but not last gasp. You didn't fight it.

Did you know I wasn't coming with you? Could you feel me dragging behind?

When we first met, you told me about your favourite saying, something about an old proverb that a kiss was a mingling of souls, and now that we'd kissed we'd be in each other forever.

You've kept your hair long: spider's silk between my knuckles. I expected mold and the same degree of decay that's been around me since the first sky went out. You still smell like incense and ink, blue ballpoint pen and black magic marker.

I grip the back of your hair now like I should have then. If I'd held on maybe it would have worked. How do you work your way back into someone's life when there's hardly any life left?

I'll still hold on to you but you need to know that there's someone else I want to be holding onto soon.

In a dream attached to a dream Anadin's voice rises up from underwater. "Don't look at the lake too long," she says. "The dregs at the bottom will suck you in with it. Just wake. Wake up."

My stomach is empty again. I make a pile of stale saltines I stole from the old lady's house and eat them one at a time. The crackers are so old they've gone soft but I shove them in anyway until they're a wad at the back of my tongue and a rock in my gut.

It's hotter today than yesterday but I keep telling myself, "Ride." I mumble it when I can spare the breath: "Ride, ride, ride." I don't let myself stop until a headache arcs sharply between my ears. There's a road motel off to the right. I manage to get into the parking lot and off my bike before I faint.

Tara's toe is in my rib, the steel of her boot enough to bruise. The reality is as unexpectedly crushing as her greeting.

"What are *you* doing here?" she asks, the "you" heavy with déjà vu.

It's still day but over Tara's shoulder I can see the moon hanging heavy and full, closer to the Earth than I've seen it yet. A vertical grin smirks from a crack in its belly.

"Did you know what I was thinking?" Tara asks, kneeling beside me. "I was thinking that I couldn't do this without you. I couldn't be here alone. You must have gotten into my head and heard me."

A chunk of moon falls toward the dead of the lake. It doesn't take speed; its plummet is slow, a featherweight rock. There's no rush. The End is already here and wants to take its time with the process.

There was a time when the moon was considered a good omen. When far, it meant an exposure of secrets, which isn't always as bad as it sounds. But rules have reverted now, turned in on themselves.

Tara's cheeks have broken out under the skin. A tiny white worm pokes its head out of her right nostril. She wipes at it with the back of an arm and then puts out her hands to help me up. We go slow but my head still spins.

Tara's been living in this motel since she left the house. Neither of us knows how many days it's been. I don't ask. A fox, dead for maybe three days, is in the parking spot in front of Tara's room. I can see it from here, its mouth unhinged, tongue shriveled. Tara shows me its tail that she cut off.

"It came away clean, no blood," she says. "I just had to shake it out in case there were fleas or something." She's been keeping it in her bag, leaving its white tip peeking out.

The curtains on the window of Tara's room have been torn off and left on the floor. There's a knock on the door. "Just a minute," Tara says, and then to me, "Come next door. Colton's gonna hook me up. You want some?"

Tara walks ahead of me and I follow her out. The room two doors down still has its curtains and its darkness expands around us.

"Who's that?" Colton asks, pointing at me but looking at Tara.

"That's my friend, Ang," she says. "Remember, the girl I told you about?"

"She's not planning on staying here is she?"

"No," I say. "I'm just visiting. Heading east from here."

Colton's counting out some doses of grayline. He stretches back onto the bed and pats the space beside him. Tara moves in, runs a hand down his thigh. Their weight against the headboard of the bed sends a light brown spider squirming out from behind it. The spider runs up the wall and into a thick web in the corner where other spiders are at work on white sacks with dark, squirming middles.

"How much grayline have you got today?" Tara asks.

"Some," he says. "How good are you gonna be today?"

"As good as you need me to be. But you've got to give some to Ang, too."

Colton doesn't take money. I offer but he says company is his currency. Tara leaves the room for a second to get some air and he says, "I'm getting bored of looking at her when I tell my stories. And she never has much of anything to say, which is why she's always touching me. I'd like to talk to you, though. Look at you. You want to look at me?"

He tells the stories of each of his tattoos: a scythe, a fish, a sun, a star. He tells the stories of his scars: surgery, fight, car accident, motorcycle accident, grease fire, cigarette burn.

Tara returns, out of her head. She starts nodding out almost right away. Her chin sinks into her chest and a small wet circle of drool appears on her shirt. A spider crawls over her shoulder and through the warm spit, disappears into her mouth.

"You want a candy?" Colton asks. He holds out three lollipops: yellow, red, orange. I go for the yellow one. It hits my front tooth and the rush of synthetic lemon mixes plaque and the copper under-taste of blood. I don't want Colton to know I just knocked out my tooth and that it's now gnawing its way through me.

"Is the grayline on you yet?" he asks, eyes half-shut. Tara swallowed most of it so I'm not expecting much, but a soft wave kicks in just as he gets me thinking about it, as if it needed my permission to flow. Euphoria slowly rises through my chest, just as Colton nods off.

I lie back, too, and try to re-create my earlier dreams, but the pain in my gums flutters through the gap where my tooth used to be and keeps me distracted. I unwrap a red lollipop that's fallen onto the floor and rub it against my bare gum as if it will make it feel better. My stomach aches and I wonder if it's working against the edges of the tooth.

There's more drowsiness with this grayline than what I'm used to. It must be cut with something but I can't place what that might be.

When I wake again my tooth has grown back. I had no dreams while I slept through the pain of teething and the ache in my stomach is gone. I wonder if my body pushed out fresh bone or if the tooth just found its way back to where it belonged.

Tara's head is still on her chest, but she's slumped slightly sideways. The drool on her shirt has expanded into a small pool of thin vomit. Even in the dank light of the room I can see her skin's gone grey, a colour I know from Aimee's adoption of death.

"Shit," I say, and then remember we aren't alone. I peek over the top of the bed but Colton's still asleep.

On my knees in front of Tara I say, "Wake up," even though I know she won't. I try to reach into her thoughts but can't. I lay her on her side. Her cheek is hard under my lips. I want to whisper something to her but don't know what to say, so my mouth just pushes out silence.

The nightstand drawer is full of lollipops. I grab them in handfuls and put them in my bag to take with me. And then I see Tara's bag, and I take that, too.

I test my strength before getting back on my bike by clenching and unclenching my fists. I can't faint again because there's no one left on this road who I can trust to help me. I make a note of the weakness in my hands. Clench, unclench. The heel of my palm is pocked with crescent moons. My skin is stuffed under my fingernails, handlebars holding chunks of my palms. My body is decomposing already, before my heart or my head have even stopped. I rub at the eye earring Tooth gave me and think, *Maybe it'll go away once I get there.*

Outside the sun's still strong enough to cast shadows. As I pull out on my bike, I see the silhouette of Tara's foxtail bobbing behind me.

On the highway I rush underneath overpasses. Their concrete torsos have fallen away, showing off rusting metal ribcages of the road. Metal barriers have come loose and swing low. I pass a sign that says I've only got twenty kilometers to go until Montreal. I suck on one lollipop after another, keeping as much sugar in my blood as I can until I get there.

I suck on two lollipops at a time and almost swallow my tongue. I brush the hair out of my eyes and a hundred strands come away in my hand. I wipe my nose with the back of my hand and it ends up smeared with watery blood. I catch my foot on the road when my sole slips from the pedal and I feel a toenail come loose. I think of Tara, feel for a psychic connection, just in case I was wrong to leave her, but get nothing back.

At Montreal's outer limits the sun is still in the same position as when I left the motel. I wonder if we'll have to wait another day for night to come.

I stop ahead of an overpass to catch my breath, rest my legs. It's the first break I've taken. Spraypainted in neon orange on the side of the bridge is a greeting:

WELCOME TO THE END OF THE WORLD

The paint isn't fresh, but it throbs with accuracy. With my front wheel facing east, I ride.

Acknowledgements

Thank you to Kire Paputts, my favourite person, who always lets me disappear when I need to get some writing done, and who read several versions of this story along the way.

Thank you to Danila Botha, Shanen Crandon, Jason E. Hodges, Marisa Iacobucci, Misha Lobo, Ken Rodney, and Natalie Zina Walschots for reading this novel in its developing stages and providing valuable feedback, support, and, most of all, encouragement.

Shanen Crandon also deserves credit as the source of the Ouija board story that appears on page 43.

Thank you to Jennifer Chivers, Lindsey Clark, Jennifer Clipsham, Jessica Dennis, and Cailey Lenehan, for all of the time we've known each other.

Thank you to Corpusse for the conversation, inspiration, and friendship.

Thank you to coffee, Toronto, Hamilton, wolves, Rozz Williams, and Cocteau Twins.

Thank you—big time—to Chris Needham and the team at Now Or Never Publishing for making this weird book happen.

And of course, thank you to my parents, Mary and Nelson Worth.